Dear Reader:

As 1981 draws to a close amid holiday bustle and good cheer, the SECOND CHANCE AT LOVE staff wants to thank you, the reader, for making this an exciting year for us. Your enthusiastic letters and strong support have made our venture into romance a tremendous success.

Now, as we look forward to 1982, we are happy to announce the expansion of the SECOND CHANCE AT LOVE line to include six romances each month beginning in January. You will experience the thrill and the torment, the promise and the fulfillment of true love in every one of our special stories each month.

From all of us at Jove to you, best wishes for a wonderful holiday season and a New Year filled with peace, hope and happiness.

Sincerely,

Carolyn Nichols
SECOND CHANCE AT LOVE
Jove Publications, Inc.
200 Madison Avenue
New York, New York 10016

MAYAN ENCHANTMENT

LILA FORD

A JOVE BOOK

MAYAN ENCHANTMENT

First Jove edition published December 1981

First printing

Printed in the United States of America

Jove books are published by Jove Publications, Inc.,
200 Madison Avenue, New York, NY 10016

CHAPTER ONE

ALEX BALANCED HERSELF as the small double-engined Beechcraft banked for the landing. How different this plane was from the wide-bodied jet that had zoomed her into Mexico City from Los Angeles. The pilot of the smaller plane had met her at the airport, and she was now his only passenger, along with the mailbags to be put down on the crude airstrip of San Pablo, a coastal village on the gulf, which she had been unable to find on any map.

A hasty glance toward the rear of the plane reassured her that her diving gear had not shifted. She then fumbled in her handbag for her mirror and carefully began to comb back her short blond hair as severely as possible. With a tissue she removed all traces of her lipstick. She hated herself for this sop to her fear of being fired before she was properly hired, but she wanted this job badly, and instinctively knew that being an attractive twenty-six-year-old woman was going to hinder her. As she smoothed her fashionable but businesslike safari-style outfit, she again felt how imperative it was that she get a change from California after the fiasco of the break-up of her marriage to Conrad. She was experiencing a disorientation that only a divorce could give. A change of scene, of people, of work, even of country was what she needed at this point in her life. If only this Victor Clarke would take her on.

The president of her diving group had shown her his letter, and with a pang of joy Alex had realized that of all the eligible pros belonging to the club, she was the one he would recommend. No mention had been made of her sex. Long ago her full name, Alexandra, had been shortened to Alex, a natural nickname that could not be considered cheating. Though only the slightest hint was given concerning what she would be diving for, she was sure her experience would be useful, since Clarke was an archeologist. In any case, in this day of women's lib, sex should not matter. The signed contract in her bag gave her some clout, but still the pilot's look of surprise and knowing grin when he discovered he was to pick up a woman foreshadowed what she could expect from the man she hoped would be her boss.

After a smooth landing, the plane rolled to a stop. Through the small window she saw the tall figure of a man striding toward them. The door flipped back, and the pilot jumped out, turning to help her down. They both moved aside to let the lone airport attendant enter the plane to deal with the mailbags and her luggage.

"Hi, there, Vic," the pilot greeted as the man drew closer. "I brought your diver along in very good shape," he added with a meaningful grin.

Alex felt her heart sink as her prospective boss stopped in his tracks and stared—an expected reaction. She decided she would match his gaze, and noted that the slanting rays of the sunset revealed a tall, lean and bronzed man in his early thirties. There was a purposeful quality in his muscular body which his jeans and open-throated cotton shirt could not hide—all underlined by an unsmiling face with direct dark eyes. His clipped black hair was streaked in places by the strong Mexican sun and salt water, proclaiming exposure to the elements she knew so well. She was heartened. He was certainly more dedicated than Conrad, a playboy diving for a lark.

He resumed walking toward them slowly. *"You—you're* Alex Wood?" He was frowning furiously. "My diver? You've *got* to be kidding! What the hell kind of a joke is this?"

Alex fought to make her voice sound calm. "No joke, really. I'm Alex Wood," she replied, "and I gather you're Victor Clarke." She removed her sunglasses to reveal blue eyes, which tended to nullify the severity of her combed-back hair.

"Oh, hell!" he murmured, half turning away, "I didn't ask for some Hollywood-type starlet. I need a real pro diver—I've got something important on hand."

The pilot, still grinning, reluctantly left them to see to his plane.

Victor Clarke's attack on her professionalism inflamed Alex, though she still fought to control herself. "I'm probably not what you expected, but I didn't realize I had to specify my sex in today's job market. *You* didn't, by the way—in our contract, I mean!" Her blue eyes flashed as they met his burning dark ones.

"Never mind that!" His face hardened even more.

"But I do mind—especially being called 'some Hollywood-type starlet.' You asked for the most experienced pro, and that's what they sent you. You've got my references. I've even run my own company!"

"I'll take your bag," he said abruptly, reaching for the small overnight case she carried. "I see Paco's putting your gear in the jeep. Let's get away from *here*, anyway!" She followed him to the vehicle.

A silent ten-minute ride in the battered machine brought them up in front of a one-story adobe house with a small front garden overlooking the sea.

"We didn't need that discussion in front of Bill and Paco," he said to her as they left the car and started for the front door, which, she noted, was unlocked.

She did not reply as she followed him, surreptitiously brushing back her hair, which had curled during the wind-blown jeep ride. She wanted to appear as serious and businesslike as possible, for it seemed that Vic Clarke was like all the others. Just because she wasn't downright ugly and rawboned, why was her ability doubted? She bit her lip in mild frustration as they entered a room of stark simplicity. A small wooden table with chairs occupied the center and she quickly noted a screened-off alcove for sleeping, tiled floors scrubbed to a gleam and white net curtains. Simple, functional, the room was a pleasant change from Conrad's haunts, always cluttered with a rich-man's toys.

"Now, look here," Vic began as they both sat down at the table, "I'm onto one of the most important finds of my life—not just my life, but maybe of this decade. I'm really a land archeologist, but by sheer luck, combined with a lot of common sense and research, I made an important find while diving for fun on my supposed vacation."

"I gathered as much. About a find, I mean. I've had—"

"And the brutal facts are," he interrupted before she could even mention her qualifications, seeming determined to keep her silent, "that I really need a pro—and I need a man! We have to live and work practically in each other's pockets. You probably thought I was diving for something romantic—maybe a galleon—gold coins. And maybe you thought I had a big crew, lots of divers working for me, too."

She drew herself up straight and looked him in the eye. "Isn't the truth merely that you don't want a *woman* diver?"

"Not really," he was quick to reply. "I've studied and worked with women all my life on various sites in the field—digs. But you—" For the first time he hesitated. "Well, the way I read you is—just out of the beauty shop, hair cut and styled by Mr. Kenneth or Mr. Whoever, nails all shaped, chic traveling suit for the tropics, fitted to the inch."

Again his attitude made her angry. "Don't bother to go on! What you're saying is that an attractive woman can't be efficient. You'd accept some dowdy fright, I suppose, clumping around in size-nine oxfords. Well, Mr. Clarke, we've got a signed contract, remember? And at my minimum rate, I may add, because I was tired of laying cables, dynamiting for construction—all that. On a couple of vacations I took a busman's holiday with the CEDAM Club—"

She'd caught his interest. "You mean *Club de Exploraciónes y Deportes Acuáticos de México?* The archeological diving club? They let you work with them?" His intense dark eyes studied her, but somehow she felt more than surprise in his gaze.

"Yes, they did! And we brought up anchors and cannons from *El Matancero*. I've been reef-diving since I was fifteen."

His eyes were still fixed on her, disconcerting her. But as he made no further comment, she continued after a slight pause. "What I'm getting at is I could hold you to your contract, but I won't. I don't need any active antagonism at this period in my life. I was recommended to you as the best person for the job. I came here because I wanted a change—and because I happen to prefer archeological diving. I read about Edward Herbert Thompson, the first underwater archeologist, when I was in high school and have studied every account of his explorations of the sacred wells near the Mayan ruins of Chichén Itzá. The Mayan culture has always fascinated me—especially the sacred *cenote*, or wells, in which the Mayans made human sacrifices to the water god, Yum Chac. When I heard about this job, it seemed like a perfect opportunity to learn first-hand a great deal more about Mayan civilization." She stopped abruptly, somewhat embarrassed at having let her enthusiasm run away with her.

But her knowledge seemed to have impressed the quietly powerful man across from her. "You say you had your own company?" he asked as he rose and headed for the kitchen alcove to make some instant coffee. She was again struck by the sense of purpose his every move conveyed, and she breathed a quick sigh of relief. Perhaps she'd managed to convince him she was serious.

"Yes," she replied. "It was a small company and was going great for a while, but then—" Abruptly she stopped herself. There was no need to mention how Conrad had ruined it by spending most of his time diving for shells, spearing fish—and chasing women. Given what Vic seemed to believe about women, he'd only think she was making a bid for sympathy.

He served the coffee silently and she drank, grateful for something to do to evade that unwavering, almost accusing stare, which implied that she was guilty of some actual fraud. After all, she had the necessary experience and the know-how. Was she to be punished because she was decently dressed?

"Well, since you seem to know about the field, and about the Mayans in particular, let me give you the details," he said, "though I'm sure you won't like them. This is no California Big Sur picnic, I assure you. Take the accommodations, for instance. I rented another shack like this down the road for my supposedly male diver. There's just a two-burner oil stove like here, and no hot water—only a cold shower you have to pull with a cord—"

Her eyes became bright. If this was how he meant to discourage her, he had another thing coming. "A shower!" she exclaimed. "A shower would be sheer luxury compared to what I'm used to on a job."

Judging by his expression, she thought he would try another tack—and she was right.

"Now I'm really going to level with you," he said. "It's quite possible I can't even finish paying a diver. Most of my money went to take a year off to finish my thesis on a much-delayed doctorate."

"Doctorate?"

"Yes. Archeology, of course—but land archeology."

Suddenly her concern for ensuring her job was overpowered by a desire to know more about this intriguing man. "Somehow you don't seem like an academic," she said.

"My friends tell me I'm more like a beachcomber. Well, that's what sun and salt water do for you. Leathery skin and streaked hair."

She began to evaluate him again and almost immediately realized that he was aware of it—his brown eyes locking onto hers as he caught her gaze. She found herself growing warm, and was annoyed at her reaction. Her pulse raced from the effect of his strong features.

He was really handsome, she marveled, accustomed to a prettier, Hollywood type of man. He was bronzed even down to his chest, revealed by his deeply opened shirt. His biceps, half visible beneath the short sleeves, seemed as hard and polished as those of a gymnast. Why did this man unsettle her? She had seen other attractive men—had practically grown up in bathing suits in California along with them, and never had she reacted this way. Get a grip on yourself, Alex, she cautioned.

She finally recovered enough to summon a casual quip, hoping to cover up her confusion.

"You strike me more like the lyrics of that song—an 'around the world in a plane, settled revolutions in Spain' sort of person."

"Well, thanks," he answered dryly. "But all my traveling has been geared to my work...field trips on museum expeditions—a different sort of thing. And now I think I've discovered a city that was inundated centuries ago. And I'm selfish about my find. If I applied for a grant right away, I'd have to let the world in on it too soon. I did my thesis on the Mayan culture and I've got the chance to really contribute to our knowledge of it. Once I've explored the place, found out for sure what's under that silt and sand, *then* I'll announce my discovery, apply for a grant, and head the expedition with the equipment and boats needed."

"Plus get government permission," she reminded him.

"Exactly. You see, being accustomed to land digs, I naturally thought diving was fun. But I now have to make hundreds of dives—and alone, from my little forty-footer, *Vera,* with a one-man crew, Pepe. That's why I need help. God only knows what I'll find there—what I might be able to bring up. I've only done cursory exploration, seen what might be remnants of streets, and maybe buildings. I haven't yet been able to date it. But the location suggests an old Mayan city flooded perhaps a millennium or so back...perhaps by a tidal wave—who knows."

She caught his growing enthusiasm. This job promised even more than she had hoped for. It was hard to restrain herself from saying, that wouldn't be hard for *me!* You've got to take me on! Never mind the money! Yet in the face of his antagonism she knew this approach would never work. She realized, however, that she possessed a powerful trump card. She listened patiently as he continued.

"After all these months of hard work, I don't plan to have everything ruined. In town they think I'm diving for wrecked galleons, and I've had to be careful as hell not to let them think I've found one. I've got something worth more than gold."

"So it seems," she agreed. "And whatever happens, I'll keep quiet about it, even if you decide not to take me on. The spoilers are all over—the Yucatan, the Mediterranean—everywhere." She paused and looked out of the window at the now fast-fading sunset. Now was the time to play her hand. "Too bad you want to find a different diver," she said casually. "You won't be able to take advantage of the specially built underwater cameras I brought along."

"You do that work?" he asked sharply. The sudden tensing of his body told her her plan would work.

"Of course! What's the use of diving unless you record some of that wonderful world down there? Whoever said that one picture was worth a thousand words knew what it was all about. Nothing like solid proof of these finds, is there? And of course you need to have a record of a significant artifact in its special place before you disturb it, remove it, bring it to the surface. Would you like to see a few of my Caribbean shots?" She finished her coffee and smiled, almost sure now of her success.

"You've got your week!" he conceded, rising. "That does it. Two skills in one—diver, underwater photographer—one salary. Maybe it will work. Come on. I'll show you to your *casita*, if I dare refer to the shack as a little house. Your gear can stay here for now. We'll go to the *zocalo*—the main square—and eat. The gang will be there by now, I guess."

"Gang?" From his conversation, a "gang" of friends, people who would possibly talk about his find, was the last thing she expected.

"Some friends I have. We usually meet for dinner. They're Americans establishing a branch here—a tool factory. I've got to speak English with somebody sometime! Let's go."

Her assigned dwelling, also facing the sea, resembled his—almost bare but spotless.

"It's the best bargain I've got here," he said when she spoke of its cleanliness. "A woman comes from the village to clean it and then water the garden. And the price is right!"

It took her only minutes to unpack the few things in her overnight bag. She was both pleased and relieved that she and Vic seemed to be getting on better. Thinking of the group she would soon meet, she changed into the only dress she had brought along, a strapless sheer cotton for summer evenings, a dress that demanded the high-heeled strap sandals she had thought to include. With a touch of lipstick and a quick hair-comb, this time with deference to its styling, she completed her preparations.

"Ready!" she announced, returning to the living

area. "Hope I won't embarrass you in front of your friends. Haven't had time to shake out the wrinkles, if any."

He gazed at her speechless for seconds, his eyes sweeping from her head to her sandals. The hostility returned full force. "Just a minute, please," he said curtly. "First I'd better lay down some ground rules." The new note in his voice and the almost piercing eyes riveted her. Even with the small table between them, he seemed to tower over her.

"If you still want this job," he began, emphasizing each word, "and if you work out okay, you've got it. But let's get a few things straight right now. You're turning out just the way I thought!"

"What in the world are you talking about?" The strength of his anger frightened her.

"Look, you're attractive. But there's no need to overdo it here. I want no frills. I want help down under every day, and no fooling around, understand?"

"But I *told* you—"

"You promised me lots of things. For some reason you want the job, but I don't need any complications—no personal relationships. Just understand that."

"But I told you—"

"Shut up and listen," he retorted, his face hardening. "We get out there to my boat no later than seven in the morning, so that means no late nights. We get in four working hours before that broiling sun hits us. We eat sandwiches on the boat, and after we digest them, we continue until almost sunset."

She nodded, too overwhelmed to speak.

"And another thing. Remember that ours is strictly

a business relationship. I'm no escort one way or another, get it? I want nothing to do with your personal life, and no problems to interfere with my dive—all understood?"

A quick anger rose in her. Granted, he was good-looking, but what made him think she wanted to go to bed with him? What an ego!

"I'm only telling you the rules of the game," he continued. "I've worked hard to get this thing going, and *nothing*'s going to stop me—nothing! Mixing work and a relationship with a sexy woman employee can snafu everything!"

She hesitated, unable to choose among ten cutting replies. Did wearing a simple summer dress imply she wanted him—expected him to squire her around this nothing town? What would he say if she were really dressed? Why, she could choose from any number of men back home, now that they knew she and Conrad had divorced.

"You wrote that you speak Spanish," he continued.

She nodded dumbly, hurt and angry.

"Then you'll be independent here. I'll introduce you to my friends, of course, but off my boat, I'm *me* and you're *you*. Understand?"

"I understand perfectly," she snapped back at last, "and would *you* please understand something, too. I didn't need that lecture from you. I've always worked under those terms with employers—some far more eligible than you, if I may say so!"

"I'm unimpressed. I can only speak for myself," he replied, turning for the door. "Snap off your lights and come on. No need to lock up. It's safe."

If only she could refuse to go. If only she could tell him what he could do with his job and with himself. But she was starving, and the only means of transportation into town was his jeep. Silently she followed him, further enraged to feel the beginning of tears. The humiliation of it all. Those were almost the same words she herself had used with prospective employers who had shown more of an interest in her beauty than her brains. *She* was the one who was supposed to lay down the rules. She would somehow get back at this man who seemed impervious to sarcasm.

The cool night air, laden with a hint of the sea, bathed her hot face. She got in the jeep and pointedly looked at the scenery as he drove, taking care to avoid his set profile but unable to ignore the quiet strength of his masculine presence.

CHAPTER TWO

"THIS IS OUR little zocalo—the town park," he announced as they approached the populated area. "We'll park over here and cross to the Taquito—the restaurant. It has simple food, but good booze and beer."

She chose not to answer, merely following him. A small band was playing in the latticework gazebo centered in the grassy circle. Couples were strolling through the moonlit paved walks, and children ran happily all over. He waited until she caught up, and again she noted his appraising, almost penetrating scrutiny of her.

"Look, I had to explain how it was going to be once and for all," he began as she came abreast of him. "For your good as well as for mine. It's better that way—right?"

"If I'm allowed to speak now," she replied coldly, "I'll say that I'm quite accustomed to working with people who know the boundaries of a professional relationship. I'm a pro diver, and a photographer as well. And speaking personally, I've never wanted for an escort, thank you!"

His reaction surprised her. The eyes which had never left hers became suddenly bright, and he smiled for the first time, taking her arm to guide her toward a small canopied terrace arranged with tables which were full of customers. As they crossed the street she drew away from him, only to feel a grip of steel as he retrieved her arm.

"Now, now—no sulking!" he warned, still smiling. "That's just as bad as a personal relationship. We've got to get along, you know. Just so you understand that I'm in charge and the dive comes first, last and always!"

Before she could reply, they were greeted by a group of four at one of the tables. "Here we are," they called. "Come on over, Vic. Who's your friend? Why so late?"

"Thought you were going to meet your diver at the airport!"

"Waiter," called out a large man. "Bring more chairs—*chairs*—oh, *sillas*, then. Haven't taught them English yet."

They joined the group, Vic introducing her. "These are the nice gringos who make a big American company work here," he joked. "Here's Edward Foster—Ed to friends—the boss."

He was large, the executive type, Alex quickly noted, a little overweight but obviously able to deal with a challenge.

"And Marga Towers, his assistant."

A cool brunette with classical features gave her a searching look, barely acknowledging the introduction.

"And Don and Jill Bentley," Vic finished as he sat down next to Marga.

The Bentleys were an almost identical-looking blond couple, who made room for Alex between them.

"And what happened to your diver, Vic?" Ed asked after they had ordered. "Missed the connecting mail plane?"

"She's here—sitting with us," Vic replied, enjoying their reaction.

"Oh, my God!" Ed exclaimed, resorting to a large gulp of his drink. "Don't tell me this—this *angel*'s going down there in those shark-infested waters! It's okay for you, Vic, to risk your misspent life on that pipe dream, but is it fair to drag someone like her into it?"

"You're a *diver?*" Jill Bentley asked unbelievingly.

"I have been for about eight years," Alex replied.

"But isn't it hard on the skin—drying?" Marga asked.

"Not if you know how to take care of yourself," Alex quickly told her. She didn't want this kind of talk in front of Vic.

As the evening progressed, the contrast between Marga's attitude and the warm acceptance of the others became apparent. The dark beauty's possessive arm around the back of Vic's chair told Alex everything, as did Marga's occasional low-voiced comments to him. Aha, thought Alex. *She*'s the reason for all the flack I took back there. He wanted to be sure I wouldn't cramp his style. He's probably explaining to her right now that it was a big surprise his diver turned out to be a woman. Yet despite Marga's coldness, she found it easy to enjoy the evening, since the dinner was good and her margarita was the best one she had ever tasted. She even endured without comment Vic's explanation of her presence.

"Never dreamed she'd be a woman," he said, throwing her what struck her as an almost patronizing glance. "Who was to know that anybody named Alex Wood would turn out to be feminine!"

"Sorry about that," Alex murmured.

"I started to turn her around and send her back, but my friends, I couldn't do it. We've got a contract, and quite a job ahead of us."

And *I've* got the cameras and the know-how, Alex thought. "It's not exactly fair to Vic, don't you think?" Marga asked sweetly, placing her hand in his.

"I'm a professional diver," Alex replied sharply. "That's what he asked for and that's what he got!"

Marga shot her a quick look unseen by the others—a look that seemed to declare a private war.

"I'll drink to that!" Ed declared. "You'll decorate this little group no end. You see, here in San Pablo, we aren't exactly in exile, but almost. The Mexican government wants to develop outlying regions," he explained, "so they give us the land free if we build a business in this area instead of in the Federal District. My parent company, in Massachusetts, picked me for the job...but we don't get many Americans down this way. It's nice to have a touch of home."

"And we're his right-hand staff," Don chimed in. "Mexico is just what Jill and I needed, a change of pace. Those cold New England winters were getting us down."

"Yes," Jill chimed in. "There's just something so special about this part of the world, a sense of timelessness. In fact," she said to Alex, "I've felt as if I were on my second honeymoon ever since we arrived."

"You both work in the plant?" Alex asked.

"You bet we do. We started out as college sweethearts and both got jobs at the main offices. We've worked together ever since—never a problem." Here she turned to look at her husband.

"Can't understand all that stuff about seeing too much of each other. Why, I'd be lost without Jill at home, and at the plant, too. Of course, Ed gives me a free hand with everything. We've known each other for years."

"You two reaffirm my faith in marriage," Alex said with a smile. "I'm from California, and among my friends, two marriages are almost par for the course."

"Don't tell me you've had a bad marriage, young as you are." Jill put a comforting hand on her arm.

She hesitated, her pent-up emotions giving her some inexplicable desire to confide in the only people who had given her any sort of welcome so far. Vic seemed to be preoccupied with Marga, so she felt free to speak with Ed and the Bentleys. "It comes to that," she told them. "I thought that scuba diving, surfing and running barefoot on the beach together was enough for the a stable marriage."

"Sounds pretty romantic, at any rate," Jill said.

"That's just it," admitted Alex. "Romance is not enough. Neither is charm—especially when there's too much of it. Then it gets to be too much for everybody." She thought again of the pain Conrad's infidelity had caused her.

Ed finished his drink and mercifully changed the subject, much to Alex's relief. "Now, folks," he said in a fatherly voice, "we've all got to work tomorrow.

Vic, you stop detaining my assistant. She's got to be bright and alert in the morning."

"You're the lucky ones," Vic replied. "No work until ten in the morning. Alex and I have to be up and at it by seven."

"Why do you do it, Vic?" Ed asked. "Even if you do find whatever it is you're looking for—a wreck or whatever—you've got so many government restrictions to worry about. Just ask me about government restrictions."

"But it's the challenge, and the winning," Vic replied as everyone made the move to leave. Alex noted the determined tone of his voice. "You've got your factory and I have my dream."

"Yeah. Maybe getting mentioned in somebody's master's or doctoral thesis gives you a jolt. Can't understand these archeologists. That stuff is as dry as old bones!" Ed sniffed.

"It's just those old bones we're usually looking for." Vic laughed at him. Alex could not help but notice that his arm was around Marga's waist.

Alex shook hands all around and thanked Ed especially, as he had picked up the check for all of them. She waited until Vic had said good night to Marga, and followed him, a pace behind, to the jeep, waving back to the others, who had parked in another street.

They drove back in the even fresher breeze, silent until Vic spoke. "Hope you liked my friends. Ed might be a little off-putting at first, but you can take my word for it—he's a smart businessman. He's doing a damn good job with that new factory."

"I found the Bentleys very nice—at least they welcomed me. And Ed's great—a love," she replied.

"He's tops. And Marga's great, too. You'll like her once you get to know her—you two can be good friends."

"Oh, really?" she answered, suppressing a rising anger. Praise of that woman was the last thing she wanted to hear after those cleverly concealed put-downs Marga had given her, plus her calculatingly covert glances. How blind he was. She was so caught up in her thoughts that she hadn't noticed they'd reached the *casita*.

"Here we are," he said, pulling up in front of her house. "You go in, and I'll wait until you close the door. This time you can lock it. I'll stop by for you early so you can go through your gear and get what you need."

"Good night," she snapped, to hide the fact that she was almost seething.

Again she felt the steel grip on her wrist. She jerked away, only to be caught up again. Looking up, she saw that he was smiling.

"I told you you were spoiled," he said. "There you go, sulking again."

She exploded at last. "What the hell do you want from me? You're *you* and I'm *me* off the boat, remember? Well, Mr. Self-appointed Sex Symbol, we're *off* the boat now, and *I*, for one, am keeping the distance!"

"Oh, come off it! Just because I explained my policy, you get up on your high horse. I didn't say we couldn't be friends, did I?"

"You've got plenty of friends!" she retorted, immediately regretting her words. With his ego, he might take that for jealousy.

"But I'm working with you—that's another thing entirely," he said huskily.

She glanced up at him and saw an expression she could not fathom. A slight shiver went through her as the two of them stood motionless, as if frozen, the grip on her wrist slowly relaxing.

"Let's begin again—no strings but no sulks," he finally said. "Just to show you there's no hard feelings on my part—" He bent and kissed her forehead. Then, suddenly seeming to be caught up in some strange magic, he pulled her to him, and she felt his lips hard on hers for what seemed like an eternity. She could not pull away, and gradually her resistance diminished as she relinquished herself to his embrace. When he finally released her, she fell back upon the seat, confused and shaken.

"Well, well," he said quietly. "Is it the moonlight or have I had too much to drink? Don't worry, Alex. It won't happen again."

Her senses slowly returning, she took her handbag and stumbled from the jeep, reaching the little house almost at a run. She shut the door and stood against it until she could think more clearly, and heard the sound of the motor as he pulled away to his house, farther up the road. Moonlight indeed! His quip about having had too much to drink was really just another implied insult—an excuse. All that business about no personal relationships—and then what did he do? She tried to work herself into a deeper anger, hoping to keep an unwelcome thought from surfacing. But she was finally forced to admit to herself that his kiss had aroused something in her she had never felt with Conrad. She had wanted that kiss to go on forever. What had happened to her pride? After all, she'd known him for only a few hours!

She pushed the thought back to a convenient corner of her mind and concentrated on being angry. She would certainly show him. Exactly how was not quite clear at the moment, but she was sure she would think of something effective. Damn—what a dilemma. And she'd thought this job would help her *forget* personal problems.

She hardly remembered going into the sleeping alcove and preparing for bed, to sink into a troubled slumber.

CHAPTER THREE

ALTHOUGH THE ALARM of the little travel clock buzzed softly, Alex woke with a start. The events of the evening before surged up in clear focus, slowly giving way to thoughts of the challenge of the job before her. She automatically did what professional divers always do. Jumping from bed, she was at the window in two steps, checking the sky. It was six, and although in January there was not yet much light, she could sense a dense, foggy atmosphere under the cumulus clouds. There was also a different note in the sound of the waves which broke on the cliffs in front of the house.

"Dark water today," she murmured aloud. "What luck. What a way to start!"

She showered and dressed, this time in correctly faded denims, checking the weather from time to time. Vic pulled up in front of the house just as she was opening her door to watch the cresting waves.

"Bad luck—we'll lose a day, I guess," he said as he began hauling her gear from the jeep. He acted as though he had never kissed her last night.

Glad of the diversion, she began to help him, choosing to move her cameras herself.

"Maybe not entirely lost," she replied as they began to pass each other with their loads. "We've got to synchronize our signals, and, of course, I want to be fully acquainted with any codes you and your man have established between you."

"Okay. I'll cue you in on what we do. Let's talk on the boat, since Pepe's waiting there anyway. He's got the coffee ready by now."

Half an hour later they boarded the jaunty *Vera* from the pier, where Pepe had maneuvered her. Alex immediately classed the welcoming José Juan Soto Romero, otherwise known by his nickname, Pepe, as *simpático*, noting strong, serious bronzed features as he offered his hand to help her board. On the way over, Vic had explained to her Pepe's expertise with the boat, his willingness to do any- and everything except get into the water.

"He's forty, and I'm not not even sure he can swim," Vic had commented. "I've never seen him do it. But it seems he was born to handle boats. I met him on a big-game fishing expedition for tourists. He was in charge, and his know-how impressed me—plus that great combination of politeness and dignity you find in the nationals of the area."

"How did you get him to quit and come work for you?" she had asked.

"It wasn't easy at first. But the lure of the dive and my find got to him. I doubt I pay him what he was making with those fishing tours. But he arranged for me to rent this boat, and maybe he gets a commission on it."

Now, as Vic showed her around the craft, she was impressed by how well equipped it was, perfect for the task ahead. Though only a forty-footer, it contained sleeping quarters, two decks and narrow passageways railed in along the sides. She noticed plenty of storage space for the diving gear. And the ship was attractive as well, the sunken salon where Pepe was now setting up a table, paneled in dark walnut edged by gleaming brass.

"You aren't exactly roughing it on the *Vera,*" Alex said, taking her indicated place on the banquette.

"It's adequate," Vic replied, helping Pepe with the table. "Sometimes I even spend the night here. It sleeps four comfortably."

"It's well equipped. But don't tell me Pepe fixed bacon and eggs on this rocking sea!" she exclaimed as they were served with surprising dispatch.

As the sea calmed, they were able to eat without too much trouble. Alex was surprised at her own appetite, since she hadn't really felt much like eating recently, back in California. Her spirits were definitely higher here—most likely owing, she told herself, to the fresh sea air. Pepe joined them, and they both switched to Spanish to include him.

"I'm glad Vic found some help," the older man told her. "It isn't right for him to dive alone. I am afraid for him. And even though I want to, I cannot go down there with him. I don't know anything about that kind of diving. But I do know about the boat—any boat!"

"That's what we can talk about today," Alex answered. "Just where I can fit in. We want to coordinate our work."

Pepe smiled at her and nodded as though a load had been lifted from him. Alex could see that he held himself responsible for Vic's safety, and now he had passed part of that burden onto her. She was glad to note that he never questioned her ability to undertake it.

"Women in the States can do anything," he said as though reading her mind. "I know. There was that woman who set the record for deep-sea diving—over three hundred feet. I know—I read all the papers when I go home from the boat."

"You see! There's a liberated man for you!" she exclaimed to Vic. *"He* doesn't doubt me at all!"

Vic smiled, and her heart did a small flip as his warm dark eyes looked into hers. "You're only on trial, remember."

"Agreed. But let's get down to real business. I have the feeling you've been tempting fate—all that diving alone. Anything could have happened to you down there before Pepe could have known about it." Though they were words she would have spoken to any employer in a similar situation, she felt a strange glow of pleasure inside at being able to express concern about him. She immediately tried to discount the feeling, but it remained.

"I know all that. But what else could I do? There was nobody else I could turn to before I asked for a pro."

"How deep is your find?" she asked.

"It's a little over a hundred feet."

"And you judge your rest stops?"

"By the Navy's Standard Air-Decompression Table."

"Great." She was surprised at the sense of relief she felt that he was aware of the proper techniques and so had been in less danger than she had feared. She quickly continued, "I see you know what you're doing. Most of my jobs have been with rank amateurs, who haven't followed some of the most important rules."

"I told you last night I was a land archeologist and dived just for the fun of it," he told her, "but the first thing I did was to learn the signals—and the basic rules. Of course in this case I went down alone, but there were mitigating circumstances."

"I suppose finding a sunken city could really be called a mitigating circumstance." She laughed. "Who could blame you for trying to keep your secret? Let's go through our hand signals—sometimes there's variation. Then we'll call Pepe and go through the rope signals. I want to be sure we're all coordinated. If you want to change things your way, let me know and I'll conform."

They worked and practiced all morning, at times making minor changes in the established routines. They found it easy going since they had basically the same grounding, and finally they broke for lunch, exhilarated that everyone was in agreement.

"Another gourmet meal," she commented as Pepe served consommé, stuffed peppers with a sauce, rice and pinto beans.

"I don't know how he does it on our budget," Vic replied. "He markets early every morning. I didn't know he was such a good cook when I hired him."

"You've got a deck hand, a cook and a terrific friend all in one," she told him. "It's obvious he's been trying to get you to hire another diver. I could see it on his face—the smug look when we were talking about safety measures."

Vic shrugged. "It's also a question of *dinero*—money. I had to figure my budget six ways from Sunday before I could contact your club in California. As I told you, I'm hurting. I've always wondered why there was so much of the month left at the end of the money."

"Money isn't everything—to use a new expression," she said. "Not that it's entirely unimportant."

"Just get me half of the next best thing." He laughed cynically. "I never really thought about it deeply before, being more concerned with the work and expertise I contributed to a particular dig, generally roughing it. But now, directly involved with the funding of a project, I find it's often on my mind."

"It certainly helps," she conceded, realizing that she had never wanted for it. Her family had been well off, and as a talented professional, she'd made what she needed to provide a comfortable lifestyle, and even had a good-sized savings account in California. Now that she thought about it, she realized how much Conrad's wealth had hindered rather than helped him. Too much money, a constant desire for *things*, had spoiled his character, making his true avocation that of a playboy. And now, here was Vic in need of money for a worthy project, the completion of which would yield him little, if any, material return.

She gazed at his powerful body and again marveled at the firmness of his jaw, the sense of quiet strength and determination that he projected even in repose. Could she tell him she did not need her agreed weekly salary right now, that she could wait till the end of the project? Or would he only consider that a maneuver on her part to keep the job? She decided to take the chance.

"Look," she began, keeping her eyes on her dessert lest she meet his and lose her nerve, "I meant to tell you about my salary—I usually select one of two possible means of payment even though my contract states I'm to be paid weekly."

"You want another agreement?" She looked up quickly when he spoke, and saw a flash of something—was it just anger?—in his face.

"Well, if it's all okay with you, here's what I can do. Suppose you pay me at the end of the job—when you get your grant—that is, if you do decide to keep me on?"

He studied her for a moment without speaking. For some reason which she did not want to examine, she was aware of a nervousness she would never have felt with any other employer.

"Get paid at the end of the job?" he repeated. "Why, that might take a month or more. Whoever heard of that type of arrangement?" His eyes grew hard and he continued. "Look, I might as well tell you now—you've got the job. I can see you know what you're doing, so you don't have to give me any leeway—or do me any favors."

She saw now that she had accurately judged his pride and that her offer had offended him. "I was only thinking of my habit of spending my money pretty freely in foreign countries," she improvised, almost unable to understand why she felt it was important for him not to be angry with her. "On some jobs I do get paid at the end, for that reason. But if you want to pay me weekly, I'll accept it."

"I appreciate your offer," he repeated firmly, "but no favors. Now, if you've finished, maybe we can check out the equipment." He ended abruptly, his face a dark mask.

Walking in silence, they passed Pepe on their way to the deck.

"I'm glad you're here, *Señorita,*" he called out to her. "Now I can concentrate on my own work."

What a dear, she breathed. He must have overheard their exchange—and understood from his many years of working with North Americans. He was looking out for her feelings, which was certainly more than his boss seemed to do.

"But Pepe, what difference will there be?" Vic replied in protest. "I did all the diving anyway. Your duties won't be any different than before. You'll have to be the look-out and wait for the rope signals just the same."

Pepe paused, the dirty dishes in his hands detracting in no way from his close resemblance to some ancient Mayan god. After a slight pause for effect he retorted, "Yes, but *now* I don't have to do the worrying! That's what takes up more energy than anything else, *verdad,* Señorita?" He winked at Alex, and all three of them laughed, effectively clearing the air.

"That's definitely the truth, Pepe," said Alex. "But by the way, I'm no longer a señorita, I'm a *señora.*"

"Well, you still seem young enough to be a señorita to me," Pepe replied.

Alex laughed, and was surprised to see when she turned toward Vic that his face was again dark. Oh, no, she thought, what was her crime this time—talking too much on the job? He motioned to her to follow him to the deck, and she noticed he moved well out of Pepe's earshot.

When he turned to her again, he looked so angry that she actually took a step back. He grabbed her arm and pulled her close to him. "I thought you were being straight with me," he hissed, "that your sex was the only thing you'd lied about in our correspondence. What's this about being married? What exactly have you told your husband about our work?"

She decided to ignore his remark about her having lied, since that was ground they'd already more than covered. She also knew that it was vital to keep control over herself—at the moment this project was the most important thing in the world to this man. She realized that much just from the little time she'd known him. Forcing her voice to be as steady as possible, since thoughts of Conrad only added to her discomfort and fear of Vic's anger, she told him only the briefest details. After all, her personal life, as he'd so clearly stated her first night, was none of his business.

"I'm señora because I *was* married once," she replied, willing her cobalt eyes to meet his obsidian ones. "But it's completely over—no more papers to sign, no more commitment, no more worry." She could no longer face him, and turned quickly away.

His grip relaxed and his manner softened. In fact, though his reply was gruff, she felt—or did she just imagine it?—an underlying tenderness. "I'm sorry," he said. "You caught me off guard, and I thought you meant you were still married. How old are you, anyway?"

"Twenty-six," she told him. "Now if you think I'm too young, we can go over my qualifications again."

His reaction told her he did not miss the slight bitterness in her tone. "No," he said, putting a conciliatory arm around her shoulders, "why don't we just get going and finish checking out the equipment." They walked for a few steps along the deck, his arm still around her, and she felt a sense of calm flow through her unlike any she'd felt in a long time. But it wasn't just his nearness, she assured herself. Surely the gentle, caressing sea breeze combined with the life-giving Mexican sun gave her this sense of well-being.

She did not have long to dwell on her thoughts. He seemed to feel as much as she did that a more businesslike approach was needed now, and when they reached the equipment, the two of them quickly got down to work. After half an hour's inspection and comparing notes, she suggested that he drive her back to the casita to check how her cameras had survived the flight from California.

"That's a good idea." He nodded. "I'll drop you there now and get back to the boat for a while, but I'll pick you up for dinner."

"Thanks." She smiled. "Since I don't have a car, I accept your offer this time, but when I get a little more settled, I plan to rent one. I don't want to be a burden."

"No trouble at all," he replied, surprised.

It was suddenly plain to her that the thought of her ever having her own means of transporation had not occurred to him. So that's it, she mused. He wanted to work with her in the day, see that she had dinner in the evenings and then drive her home to be sure she was tucked in for the night while he cavorted around town with the beautiful Marga. Well, she determined, he had another thing coming.

As they were driving back, he mentioned the car idea again. "I just want you to know I don't mind giving you a ride for dinner in the evenings. What I said about not being an escort doesn't apply to giving you an occasional lift."

"Thanks a lot, Vic," she replied, "but I've always had my own car. The only reason I didn't drive myself down was I didn't know what the roads were like in this part of Mexico . . . also, I didn't want to drive all that distance alone." That seemed to satisfy him, and they drove the rest of the way in silence.

She spent the afternoon carefully checking and unpacking her cameras and lighting equipment. The sound of the small drizzle, called, appropriately she now realized, "cheepy-cheepy" by the local people, was pleasant as it mixed with the more remote roar of the waves breaking on the rocks below the cliff. Her sense of well being was enhanced by the fact that both she and Vic had seemingly forgotten the events of the night before. Her own absorption in the challenge of the dive, in checking out the equipment and coordinating their signals, helped push the unexpected kiss into the background. Then there was his recognition of her know-how. He had said straight out that she knew what she was doing. The rest would be easy, without the need to prove anything. She would proceed as on any other assignment, only with a wary eye against his egotism. It wouldn't hurt him at all to be taken down a peg. The rules he had set forth the night before still rankled. Who had asked him to be her escort anyway? With her own car—which she would definitely arrange for as soon as possible—she would be independent of him and his jeep. She smiled, remembering his not being able to think of a valid reason against her having a car.

The little house now took on a homelike aspect, with her familiar things placed throughout it. The books she had brought rested on the little table beside the bed. Two small Cézanne reproductions hung in the living area. Her photographic equipment was safely stowed away, ready for transport to the boat when weather permitted.

At seven that evening the rain finally stopped, and shortly afterward Vic pulled up in front of the house. Dressed in her designer jeans, with flat-heeled sandals and a denim jacket for the rain-cooled evening, she got in beside him.

"I hope you approve," she said lightly as they pulled away.

"Approve?" He looked at her. "Oh, you mean your outfit? Yes. Very nice—very simple. That's the way we do it in San Pablo."

"I understand. But you might be interested to know that what I'm wearing now cost twice as much as what I had on last night."

"What! Just a pair of jeans?"

She laughed. "I can see you're really buried in

academia. Don't you know that jeans are a high-fashion luxury item now? Where do you buy yours?"

"In the Army-Navy stores back in the States and in the workmen's furnishing stores down here."

"Well, when you get back to the States, you're going to be surprised," she assured him. She then breathed in the fresh smell of the countryside, and again felt a welcome sense of calm.

They were the first to arrive at the restaurant. Vic ordered drinks and sat down opposite her. The others pulled up shortly and came in, Ed deliberately seating himself beside her.

"We didn't properly celebrate your arrival last night," he said as they settled down. "Who was to know we'd have an angel in our midst? I expected some big male lout—a bit on the crude side."

"There's no need to do anything special," she protested. "I had a wonderful time last night."

"But that's not the point. We're in Mexico now, and the hospitality is entirely different. You haven't had a real welcome."

Jill and Don Bentley together underlined Ed's words. Marga, now involved in a private conversation with Vic, had barely greeted her.

"But we're all so busy," Alex continued. "What kind of celebration were you thinking of?"

"Just a little something for tonight," Ed assured her, studying the menu while he sipped his drink. "Thought we might run over to Tierra Quemada—that's the next little town," he explained, "and see some flamenco. They always have a good show there, and a great orchestra for dancing. Nothing too late, mind. I want my staff to keep in good shape, but it does happen to be Friday, and we don't work tomorrow."

"But *we* do—if it doesn't blow up another *Norte,*" Vic interrupted.

"Oh, you're still with us?" Ed feigned surprise. "Thought you and Marga were in a private conference over there." Alex had to hide a smile at Ed's remark.

"Oh, let's go," Marga urged. "There's so little to do in San Pablo. You need a break, Vic. All work and no play..." She smiled archly at him. "You haven't taken me anywhere for ages!"

Alex recognized this establishing of possession. How obvious can one be, she thought. Of course, it was hard on Marga to have her very own Victor saddled with a woman diver—one who worked daily with him and lived right down the road.

"We couldn't work today because of the weather," Vic told the group, "but maybe a couple of hours won't make all that much difference."

Marga gave a joyous squeal, and Jill immediately chimed in, "Oh, great! I love my work, but there comes a time when that dull feeling creeps up on you. If I had one problem this week, I had fifty."

"Count me in," Don said dryly. "I know all about those fifty problems. Things are certainly done differently here than in the home office. It takes some getting used to."

"Agreed, then," Ed said, turning to Alex. "Shall we make it a unanimous vote?"

"Far be it from me to throw *agua* on the *fiesta!*" She laughed.

They finished dinner with an added gaiety, helped

along by an extra round of drinks. The weather had by now completely cleared, and some of the more hardy souls had ventured out into the zocalo, where the band was tuning up for the evening concert. A thin moon came out, followed by some timid stars, announcing that in all likelihood the morrow would be a good day for diving.

"Let's get going, then." Ed rose as he spoke. "Better we should take all the cars, to make things simpler going home."

Alex noticed that Marga had a hand on Vic's arm, and she knew that the dark-haired women would not welcome her presence. Ed came quickly to her resuce. "Alex," he said, "why don't you do an old man a favor and come with me to keep me company." She nodded gratefully and followed him to his car—a loden-green Mercedes. Well, she thought wryly to herself, if Marga's got the man of her dreams, at least I've got the car of mine.

The three-car caravan began the ten-mile drive to Tierra Quemada with Ed leading the way, Don and Jill following in their sleek red Jaguar and Vic and Marga trailing in the jeep.

"You see we do have a few hot spots in the area," Ed said as they drove along the narrow two-lane highway. "San Pablo has nothing but good fresh air—a great commodity these days, but Tierra Quemada has all of three night clubs."

They both laughed. She was beginning to change her first evaluation of Ed as the typical, slightly overweight executive. Not only did he have a sense of humor which at times surprised her, but on second look one could see he had been rather handsome in his youth . . . as though he had been a college football star. She suddenly wondered why the calculating Marga didn't direct more attention his way. Though he was by no means as attractive as Vic, he was clearly successful. It seemed to her that material things would definitely appeal to the always chic, dark-haired woman. Then Ed's voice broke into her thoughts.

"But the nice part is that they import entertainment from Mexico City, and at the Casa Madrid, where we're going tonight, one can always find good flamenco. Do you like flamenco? Forgot to ask you."

"I love it," she replied. "When I was in Spain, I haunted the flamenco places. I even went to Granada and saw the real thing, in the caves."

"We can chalk up something we have in common," Ed replied. "I've been a collector of flamenco records for years."

They were silent for a while as he drove through the typical landscape so often seen by her in paintings. The maguey plants dominated it, raising their pointed leaves to the stars. Occasionally a burro grazed along the road, heedless of the passing cars. Once they had to slow down until a rabbit decided which side of the road it preferred. The air seemed permeated by a faint scent of unseen wildflowers, and now and then, above the gentle purring of the motor, the sound of cicadas came through the open window on her side. Only an occasional car passed them in the other direction, and Alex got the feeling of being in the center of a quiet and lonely beauty.

They drew up, finally, in front of Casa Madrid, on

the main street of a town only a little larger than San Pablo but with a slightly more urban flavor. Marga and Vic were the first out of their car, pausing for the rest to catch up at the entrance. Alex could already hear the music, which pulsed with a slow tropical rhythm, adding to exotic atmosphere of the night fresh from the recent rain. They gathered at the door, where they were welcomed by the maître d' and led to a ringside table.

Jill immediately went off with Don to dance, and Marga pulled up Vic, nestling in his arms with a seemingly practiced gesture, regarding Alex through veiled eyes over Vic's shoulder. Seeing the closeness of the two, Alex felt a pang of jealousy surge through her. As she watched Vic's tall, athletic physique moving in perfect time to the music, his strong profile bent to catch what Marga was saying, and Marga, enfolded in those steel-muscled arms, which had held her only the night before, she turned away and tried to quell an emotion she told herself she had no right to feel. Here she was, she scolded herself, only two nights in Mexico, having known this man for a matter of hours, and already she was reacting like a schoolgirl just because of one kiss.

Ed had been studying the wine list, looking for a good champagne and trying to ignore the unhelpful suggestions of the waiter. "Never mind your margaritas," he said in a aside to her. "Let's be a little festive!"

The two couples returned to the table as the music ended, and the fanfare for the flamenco show assaulted their ears. The lights lowered even further, and in the gloom, guitars began a slow strumming, gradually building up a mounting tension to explode into the demanding, frenetic music of Andalusia. The dancers came on, swirling, tapping, shouting, clapping in a soul-stirring ecstasy of gypsy Spain.

Almost against her will Alex was caught up in the passion of the flamenco, experiencing the primitive emotions implicit in the dancing, her feelings driven by the throbbing music into the world of primary colors, primary feelings. For some reason she began to hate the way Marga leaned so possessively against Vic. Alex identified with one of the beautiful women dancers now jealously claiming her mate from the intrusion of a rival, threatening her with the stylized heel work and hand gestures, circling her, always between her and the man; and ever in the background those insistent strumming guitars sustained the almost unbearable tension of the flamenco beat. Something fundamental stirred Alex deeply as she let the music possess her, let it tell her to claim what she wanted, with no quarter given. The beat grew heavier, and as Vic shifted his position across the table, an electric shock overwhelmed her when their legs accidentally brushed beneath the table. Then suddenly the cymbals and guitars crescendoed to a climactic finish. Alex knew that a deep red flush infused her face, and she was glad that the lights were still low. She was left shaken, but recovered enough to accept Ed's invitation to dance, as the others paired off as before.

"It's nice to have somebody else to speak English with occasionally," he told her during the dance. "Don and Jill are great, but they need some time alone together. They're my right-hand executives down here, along with Marga. Vic's so damn busy with his diving every day, and whatever time he has left, Marga wants to take it."

"Are they engaged?" Alex asked, hoping she wasn't showing undue interest.

"Not yet, I don't think." Ed laughed. "But I get the feeling she'll spring the tender trap in the long run. Vic has never really said anything to me, but I know Marga. She never gives up fighting for what she wants—and she wants Vic."

"I hope they'll live happily ever after," Alex said, attempting a flippancy she did not feel.

"I don't want to lose an executive who knows all my idiosyncrasies," said Ed, "but I'm afraid that Vic may give in soon. In fact, he's probably just waiting to get this dive of his out of the way."

Ed was probably right, she realized. Once Vic established his find, he'd be able to make the commitment marriage demands—something Conrad had never been capable of.

She saw Don and Jill dancing as though they were still college sweethearts. Why hadn't she been able to find that kind of happiness? Then, to make things worse, Vic and Marga, dancing cheek to cheek, came into view. Again, unbidden, arose that unsettling discomfort inside her, a feeling she did not want to acknowledge.

He's hers, she thought, and was, long before she herself had come. In any case, she'd only known him briefly, and he often was just civil to her.

She made herself listen to Ed and appreciated his dancing, especially since he was light on his feet for his weight. He was speaking of his college days, his fraternity dances, the times when people really danced together, not in the crazy way they did now. She finally found herself enjoying the evening and was surprised when, back at the table, Ed asked for the check.

"Ed, you're a party-pooper and a kill-joy," Marga complained. She turned to Vic. "Can't we go somewhere else? The Patio Club? Pretty please?"

"Sorry, sweet," Vic replied. "You people have the whole weekend, but my diver and I will hit the deck around seven—A.M. that is!"

"You mean you'll hit the bottom around that time." Don laughed.

"That's right." Vic nodded.

"Well, after that flamenco, everything else would be tame for me anyway. I'm ready to leave if everyone else is," Ed said.

Marga gave a martyr's sigh as she smiled at them and rose to leave. "You're the boss, darling," she murmured to Vic, taking his arm. They went ahead, with the others following.

"Marga's a good sport," Ed commented to the rest. "She could use a little more fun—she works hard. She's a darn good executive who gets things done!"

Jill pretended to bristle. "I guess a gal has to be the tall, stunning model-type to get any credit around here," she said. "What about old faithful, underestimated little me?" *Brava*, thought Alex.

"But my job would be impossible without you and Don," Ed quickly assured her. "I keep telling you that all the time!" He put an arm around each of them, heading them all to the door, where Vic and Marga had stopped to wait for the others.

"I'll pick you up at seven," Vic told Alex. "Have a good sleep."

"I'll be ready," she answered. They then walked to the cars, again thanking Ed for the evening.

The ride back with Ed could have been wonderful in any other circumstances, Alex realized. But her emotions were so confused, so stimulated by the flamenco, the guitars and the newly born feeling of jealousy, that she failed to appreciate the sea, which crashed on their left, or the stunning mountains on their right. It was as though the cliffs had risen straight up from the sea, with the road carved from living rock, later to be covered with loose gravel.

With a sigh she realized how different it would be with the right person under that silver crescent moon illuminating everything as the breakers roared a few feet below them.

She was surprised to find it was only twelve-thirty when she let herself into the casita. Sleep was elusive, and almost in spite of herself, her mind began to review her short time in San Pablo. She had jumped at the chance to get away from the scene of her recent divorce in California, the job with Vic Clarke seeming the ideal way to involve herself in a complete change. Yet, when he had explained his find and the work she would be expected to do, she had wanted the job for its own sake, loving archeological diving as she did and rarely getting the chance to do it. But the best part of all was that she would help him reveal more about Mayan culture, about that stirring civilization that had worked its magic on her since her teens.

Vic's initial antagonism had seemed to ease somewhat when he recognized her professionalism. She tried to push back what she knew she must face—her attraction to him, which became ever more powerful despite her efforts to ignore it. She thought back to the kiss that had inflamed them both. Was it just the moonlit Mexican night that had caused her to want him so badly, or was it something more? Now, stop dreaming, she cautioned herself suddenly, realizing how dangerous her thoughts were. Vic Clarke, for all his devotion to his field, was probably as fickle as Conrad had been. And knowing Marga's close connection to Vic—why, even Ed said they'd get married—she was struck by a horrifying thought. Unless she resisted her silly infatuation with Vic, *she herself* would be the other woman. And wouldn't Conrad see the irony in that? she thought ruefully.

Her thoughts chased around in her brain until she was forced to turn on the light again and try to read herself to sleep. Through the lines on the page came that taunting smile of Marga's, so possessive, so confident. And what were they doing now? She had neither seen nor heard any trace of the jeep in front of the house farther up the road. Vic had refused to go to another club in Tierra Quemada, but apparently that hadn't meant he would go directly home. Marga's possessiveness, and her antagonism toward Alex, bespoke a closeness as real as the book in front of her. Vic was obviously hers.

Alex rose to plump her pillows and resettle herself, knowing that she was foolish to let her sleep be spoiled in this way. But just as she was about to drift off, the sound of the jeep's motor came from a distance, gradually growing nearer, then passing her house to stop in front of Vic's. She heard the slam of the car door, the faint footsteps leading to his shack, and finally the slam of that door.

A sense of relief flooded over her. So he was home only shortly after she had arrived. Then he really did mean to get up early, and perhaps he had simply dropped Marga home with a few parting words.

Again came the accusing thought...what in the world did his relationship with Marga mean to her personally? Had she ever before been jealous of a beautiful rival? Rival—the word shocked her. Was she now admitting that word to her consciousness? And who in fact was the rival? She herself...or Marga?

"Oh, forget it, Alex!" she exclaimed aloud as she turned off her light, disgusted with herself, and flopped over to the most comfortable position she could find.

CHAPTER FOUR

CLEAR SKIES AND the sounds of a more tranquil sea greeted Alex when she awoke. Even though the little radio predicted good weather, she had already known by the look of the sky that the sun would later come out in full force. The doubts of the night before were forgotten as a thrill of anticipation coursed through her. A buried city—sunken perhaps centuries ago. She had never dived for so rich a treasure. To be in on the first discovery would be more than wonderful.

She was terribly excited, and ready long before seven, when Vic punctually drew up at her door. Jumping out of the jeep to begin loading her cameras and gear, he greeted her casually, his brief smile giving way quickly as he tackled the job before them.

"Is this the lot?" he asked, surveying the bundles she had prepared.

"Right," she said, assuming the same businesslike tone. "You take the heavy stuff, and I'll take charge of my cameras."

They reached the boat ten minutes later, and Alex noted that Pepe was waiting on deck. Spotting them, he came down the pier to help.

"Right on time for coffee," he announced as he

relieved Alex of her cameras with a care she appreciated. "I don't like to let it stand too long—not over half an hour."

"Hope you made double this morning," Vic said. "I need it!" Probably that nightcap he might have had with Marga made him need the coffee, Alex surmised, since none of them had overdone the champagne. That and perhaps whatever might have happened afterwards at Marga's apartment, even though he did get home early. She forced herself to forget these thoughts as the three of them finished unloading. Pepe disappeared into the galley, and she heard him prepare the morning meal.

"Thought you told me there'd be only sandwiches," Alex commented as they sat on the banquette. "I smell bacon again, and that lunch we had yesterday . . ."

"I admit I was trying to discourage you," Vic said. "We always have a light breakfast and a pretty good lunch. By the time we get to the site we will have digested our food."

"Great. I can't wait to see your sunken city."

"It's phenomenal—another world," he replied with the first enthusiasm he had shown that morning.

Pepe came in with breakfast, this time a considerably lighter one than the day before. One strip of bacon, a thin slice of papaya, coffee and a piece of toast were placed before them while the cook sat down to a generous serving of scrambled eggs with bacon, refried beans and a side dish of hot chilis.

"Couldn't I have even a one-egg omelet?" Vic begged, looking at his plate.

"For lunch," Pepe answered. "But I had planned to

serve peppers stuffed with picadillo, rice and charro beans."

"You're a hard man, Pepe." Vic shook his head.

"I had a good teacher," Pepe replied. "You! If you're going diving, I can't let you commit suicide by overeating."

Vic laughed and turned to Alex. "The trouble with Pepe is that he's always right," he declared.

After an extra cup of coffee, they cast off, and Pepe edged the boat slowly out to sea. He had several secret markers, secret to all but him, he said, that would guide him unfailingly to the diving site. Alex was first on deck in her wet suit. Shortly Vic appeared in his, and she was again struck by his physique, now completely covered by the clinging foam neoprene. It revealed every muscle in what seemed to her a sculpted body, one which could have been a model for an old master. She watched as he buckled his weight belt, then suddenly she realized that he was looking at her as she leaned backward against the rail. It had not occurred to her that her own body was under appreciative scrutiny, so accustomed was she to what she called her working clothes.

"I told you you should have tried it in front of the cameras." He smiled. "You'd have it made!"

She downed a rising confusion at the first direct compliment he had given her. "Well, I was just standing here thinking," she replied, "you don't look anything like the absent-minded professor of archeology. Unless you work out every day."

"I take that for a veiled compliment," he said as he began to put on his flippers.

"It's the only kind of compliment that won't overinflate male egos." She laughed. "A woman has to be so careful these days. But if you just happened to be passing by on Sunset Boulevard, and I was tooling down the street in my Jag," she joked, "I'd be tempted to give you the wolverine whistle!"

"That's the nicest thing anyone has said to me for a while." He grinned. "I promise not to get a swelled head."

They finished putting on their accessories, leaving the air tanks and face masks for last, timing it as Pepe slowed the boat to a gentle stop.

"Don't forget our rope signals, Pepe," Vic warned. "I'll always keep you in sight, Alex, even though I'm so used to being on my own. I'll signal you if I want to explore something."

"Good. I'll be measuring the depth and figuring out bottom time. That'll leave you free to concentrate on exploring."

"Right. He's stopped completely. Let's go!"

They both flipped over backward into the blue-green water, now calmly rippling. To her surprise, Vic led her in a diagonal direction rather than straight down. Finally her wrist pressure-gauge told her they'd gone down one hundred ten feet. It was dark at that level, and she saw very little. Where is the city? she wondered.

Suddenly her flippers touched sand, and in the gloom she could barely make out an irregular area where Vic was pointing. He signaled her to follow, and slowly they "walked" for a while until she could discern various moundlike structures encrusted by coral and sand. Vic pointed farther ahead, and to her delight she saw a school of brilliantly colored fish swimming in and out of what seemed to be the remains of a stone structure. It seemed so close, but she knew that something appearing to be six feet away would in actuality be eight feet distant, owing to underwater distortion. Then, too, the light had almost disappeared at that depth. The water seemed clear and clean, but only a dull monochromatic tone predominated. She knew she had to use an exposure meter with her color film, and decided to employ the strobes when the sun reached about forty-five degrees.

They had approached what she now recognized as a built-up area. Silt and sand had layered the remains of what she hoped were remnants of stone walls, and not just natural rock ridges formed by water running over limestone plus the silica of lava and pumice. In a moment of panic, she hoped that Vic had truly found a city and had not taken various undersea formations to be the remains of one.

Under the soft sand her flippers touched a harder substance which she suspected was pure pumice. An underwater volcano at work eons ago... or an earthquake followed by volcanic action which induced some sort of tidal wave? She knew that only the scientists could establish exactly what had happened. Newly struck by the size of the project, she was acutely aware that Vic needed an entire expedition to take core samples, to check for volcanic ash, for hardened lava flows, for everything—that is, if there really had been a city there.

They went along farther in the darkness, Vic pointing out what really seemed to be the remains of embrasures which might have been openings for windows at one time—some sort of ventilation effort—an indication of something man-made. With the pictures, they could establish so much, she thought. It was almost impossible to determine much at this depth without them.

Vic scooped away some sand from one of the mounds, and she swam over to him as he made the gesture for her to examine it. Putting her gloved hand on the stone, she could feel its chill through the protection she wore. Now he was pointing, but she could see nothing unusual. She realized that because of his previous diving he was much more accustomed to the site, but she nodded as though she understood.

He turned and led her deeper into what seemed to be a maze. She signaled him to take care not to bump into any of the dangerous red coral which covered some of the structures.

Later, when she remembered to check her watch for time, she was surprised to find they had been down for thirty minutes. She gave him the surfacing signal, and together they slowly rose, stopping at the estimate levels to decompress.

They surfaced near the boat, and she was glad to see that Pepe had the deep-boarding ladder ready. Weight belts and fins came off first, then the air cylinders, which Pepe took aboard first to minimize the downward pull of the ocean on their ascent.

"You're the first person I've shown it to," Vic told her the moment he removed his face mask. "What do you think?"

"It's fantastic," she answered, reluctant to throw any doubt on his enthusiasm.

"And did you examine those stones I showed you?"

"Frankly, I wasn't able to see too much at that depth. But now I know what to do when we go down again."

He seemed suddenly aware of her skeptical tone. "You didn't see the markings? Those stones were laid by hand!"

"Are you sure?"

"Of course I'm sure. I've been probing and peering at them on all my dives. I know what's down there."

"But it's just that there're so many natural formations . . ."

"Not this one," he countered. "Wait, I'll show you something." He walked away from her as she leaned back to bask in the sun. For some reason the dive had been cold and arduous. Perhaps it was just the tension of the first real day of work.

"Take a look at these," he ordered as he returned with some objects carefully cradled in both hands.

She saw what at first glance seemed to be shapeless lumps encrusted in a mixture of hard lime and even harder sand.

"Guess you can't recognize too well what they are, not having been trained to," he said as she silently examined the lot.

"What could they be? Did you bring them up?"

"Yes, and there's more down there to prove my theory," he replied. "Don't you recognize the god Chac? The great god Chac? Here's one of his likenesses . . . the same likeness that was brought up and authenticated by CEDAM on the Bush expedition to the cenote—the sacred well in the Yucatan. You say you dived with them."

She was seized with excitement. Of course! She remembered the photographs taken on that expedition. Vic was right—and she now held the likeness of a Mayan god in her hand. She could not speak.

"And the rest of these are artifacts of home life at that time, though I haven't identified them completely," he continued. "I want a professional cleaning job. Don't want to risk ruining them."

"Then it's true! You really *have* found a city!" Alex began to dance around the deck excitedly, forgetting her decision to be businesslike and formal with him.

He watched her, seemingly amused for a moment. "About an hour and a half to our next dive?" he finally asked.

"That's what I figured, too. By the way, do you have a good supply of air tanks?"

"Absolutely," he replied. "That was the first item in my budget aside from the boat. Thank goodness we can always get them from Tierra Quemada."

They dived until lunch. Then they changed into their jeans and hungrily attacked the food. Pepe, sensing their exhaustion and tension, would not allow them to help him with anything. Again Alex was amazed by her appetite.

"Think we can do any shooting today?" Vic asked as they sat in the brilliant sunlight, sipping espresso coffee.

"Yes, the sun will be great for it between one and four, I think, now that we've missed the good hours from ten to twelve. I wanted to get the layout first before I started. By the way, why did you lead me there at an angle rather than straight downward?"

His features tensed. "I meant to tell you about that. We do everything to throw off anyone who gets too interested. The people in town have the idea I'm diving for treasure, and every week we try to put down a marker in another spot. By now I'm used to the terrain in that area down there and can locate it without pinpointing it from above. Pepe also has his secret landmarks to guide the boat to the spot. And we purposely undershoot and overshoot at times."

"Now I understand. Hope they don't spy too much, or you'll have the spoilers in your hair."

"Exactly," he agreed. "As a matter of fact, I take one day and go in an entirely opposite direction. We lose the day, but at least it helps keep them at bay."

"Who would these people be?"

"Oh, boys from the town, for one. They're terrific swimmers and would maybe even try free-diving, for a lark, at that depth. They'd thrash around down there and just about ruin everything! Gold-crazed, they'd root around for some phantom Spanish galleon! And then, of course," he continued, "we have to contend with the gringo college kids on vacation. But this kind of talk is depressing." He flashed her a smile. "Let's get back to work."

The afternoon dives continued, with Alex shooting pictures. As the strobes revealed the fantastic underwater colors as well as proof of Vic's theory, she felt she had entered an enchanted silent domain. Using the slowest possible film to get a finer-grained result, she patiently waited until the sand they had stirred up preparing for each shot had settled before she took another.

First Vic led her to the areas he most wanted, and she made two shots of each section, occasionally having to resist the temptation to catch a school of gaudily colored, wise-looking angel fish following their every move. The two passed a busy afternoon and barely kept within the bottom-time limits. Alex couldn't remember a more interesting day in all her diving experience and felt a sense of disappointment when Vic led her back to the ship after their last dive.

"Do you think you've got anything good?" was the first question he asked her after boarding. He studied her intently, and she felt a sense of excitement that she had to admit was not related to the diving. She was melting inside and had to struggle for control.

"I'm sure I did," she managed to assure him. "I used my best and slowest film, and my magenta filter to compensate for that hot blue light the strobes give out. And thank heaven we didn't get a high-voltage jolt from those strobes!"

"And what about developing them?" he asked, the same unsettling look still reaching into her soul. Combined with his businesslike questions, it confused her. Had Conrad's lack of regard led her to weigh any handsome man's attention to her, even in a job situation, more heavily than she should?

"Don't worry," she replied. "I've got my trusty little traveling kit, which I'll set up tonight."

She knew she should go below now to change out of her wet suit, but she seemed rooted to the spot. As the soft sea breeze blew over them, they lingered on the deck, and for a thrilling instant she thought he was going to kiss her again. He leaned toward her, and Marga or no Marga, she knew she would not refuse his embrace. Then suddenly he seemed to catch himself and drew back. Had he just thought of Marga as well?

She was not able to ponder the question long, for just then Pepe clambered up to the deck. Vic turned suddenly. "We'd better hurry so we'll be in town in time for dinner with the others," he told her as he headed for the stairs. So, she thought bitterly. Marga *was* on his mind.

Though Pepe took a different route home this time—a prettier one, he told Alex, so she could see the more beautiful parts of the coast—she did not feel any magic. Vic had remained below.

CHAPTER FIVE

THAT EVENING THEY were only five at dinner, as Alex and Vic were told that Ed had had to fly to Boston for the weekend. Though Jill and Don wore their usual clothes, Alex was surprised to see Marga in a blue ruffled organdy dress with matching shoes. She seemed ready for a party.

"I thought I could get you in a real Saturday mood," she told Vic when he commented on her dress. "I just don't feel like going back to my lonely apartment on Saturday night."

"Would you like to come over to our house for drinks and then listen to some music?" Jill invited.

"Oh, how sweet of you," Marga responded, the underlying sarcasm in her voice apparent to Alex. "But what I want is more dancing. God, this town is dead. And Tierra Quemada isn't much better."

"What do you have in mind, Marga?" Vic asked.

"Well, I thought the least we could do is to check out another place in Tierra Quemada—El Patio. They've got a swinging new show and an orchestra."

"I've had a hard week," Don declared. "I enjoyed last night, but it's the beach for me tomorrow. And early bed tonight." Jill nodded in agreement.

"Then it's just up to us to decide, Vic," Marga said, turning to him.

Alex wasn't surprised to see what a nonentity Marga had made of her. Then she quickly scolded herself. After all, the woman was practically engaged to him, so why should she expect to be included in their plans? She turned her attention back to Marga's campaign.

"But we went out last night," Vic was telling Marga in a firm voice, "and I'm going to take tomorrow off to go to the beach. I hate to disappoint you, but for me, it's a drink with Jill and Don, and that's it till tomorrow."

Turned down in front of the others, Marga was forced to be gracious, much to Alex's secret amusement. All of a sudden Marga seemed to remember Alex's presence and crooned to Vic in a soothing tone, "Well, if you're tired"—and she placed a languishing hand on his shoulder—"poor Alex, here, must be exhausted. Why don't we take her home right away?"

Alex would have loved to tell them that Marga's concern was misplaced, but it was true that she wanted to be home before it got too late—not to rest, but to develop the first shots she'd taken of the secret Mayan city.

It was past midnight before she had finished, but she had some shots which she knew were good. With sufficient light and the special film, she had excelled. Maybe with a few more of these, Vic could announce his find to the world. She hung up her prints on a makeshift clothesline to dry and, finally realizing just how tired she was, prepared for bed.

Moments after turning off her lamp, she heard the jeep approaching. It slowed in front of her house, and she quickly turned on the light. She knew that Vic would be anxious to see the photos. Even an expert sometimes had bad luck with the cameras, and he would want to know. A soft knock came, followed by the deep tones of his voice, identifying himself. Quickly throwing a pale-blue silk robe over her sheer nightgown, Alex let him in.

"Please excuse the intrusion, Alex, but I couldn't wait to see the shots. I saw your light and . . ." Suddenty he stopped in his tracks. She felt herself blush a deep red as his eyes moved over her body, lingering where her taut breasts were partly revealed by the flimsy gown. Instinctively she pulled the robe around her, then folded her arms under her breasts. When she could bear to look at him again, she was annoyed to see a bemused expression on his face. He was obviously pleased at her discomfort.

"I—I heard the jeep," she said too quickly. "I thought you'd like to see what I had—" She stopped, flustered, and his expression turned into an outright grin. "I mean, how the pictures had turned out." Damn, she thought to herself. She bet he'd enjoyed that slip of the tongue.

She turned briskly to the line where the pictures hung, determined to be the coolest, most professional person ever to conduct archeological business in a silk peignoir. Why, oh, why hadn't she gotten rid of these leftovers from her trousseau at the same time that she'd signed the final papers that freed her from her extravagant ex-husband?

Thankfully she noted that the pictures had dried sufficiently to be examined, and she didn't kid herself—certainly he'd be more interested in these shots right now than in anyone's body.

She was almost right, she later noted ruefully. But at least they drew his attention away from her almost-unclothed state before she was made to blush again. "This is stunning!" he exclaimed, examining the first one. "And it's so important that we can see those deep ridges in the stones. You're quite a photographer." Though she was fully aware of her skill, she glowed at his praise. She was further gratified as he continued to look at the shots, remarking from time to time that they showed exactly what he had hoped they would. He also expressed pleasure at the quality of the photographs she'd taken of the various artifacts he'd already salvaged.

Finally he rose to leave, and she went to see him out. "How could I ever have doubted you, Alex Wood?" he said. "You're a real pro—" and again his eyes roved over her, "every inch of you."

He stopped before they reached the door, and she felt an almost otherworldly stillness, the sound of the nearby sea dwarfed by the rise and fall of their breathing. She could not deny it—there was something nearly palpable between them. She glanced up and met his steady gaze. The deep brown eyes which had often seemed so cool were inviting her to lose herself in their deep, mysterious pools. In a moment she found herself in his arms, all thoughts of Marga and his past insolence cast out of her mind. All she knew was that this was what she wanted, needed.

He held her, first gently, then in a crushing embrace as his kisses covered her face, moving to her mouth and becoming ever more insistent, more demanding.

Then he became gentle again, and a thrill of excitement surged through Alex as he started to caress one of her breasts. Slowly, deliberately, possessively he kissed her, as if he had every right to her.

She forced herself to pull away, though her body ached for him. "I think you'd better go." Her voice was tremulous. "Remember our agreement."

Again that bemused look was on his face. "As you wish," he said huskily, but before he could continue, the slow purring of a motor came to them above the sound of the waves against the cliffs. A door slammed and footsteps approached, crunching on the gravel of the walk. Vic moved away from her and opened the door to admit a wind-blown Marga.

"Oh, Vic," she sighed, falling into his arms, a pouty, helpless expression on her face. "I'm so sorry to disturb you while you're working." She moved a hand up along the front of his shirt, at the same time casting an arch look at Alex, one which spoke much better than words of *her* right to touch him. "I was so worried, because you'd left these in my car." She handed him a leather case which obviously contained field glasses.

"Well, I certainly appreciate your concern," he told her, "but I'm afraid these aren't mine. All this kind of thing is kept on the boat, since I really have no need for it here."

Concern! Was he really so blind as to not see how she just hit on the flimsiest excuse to check up on him, to make sure he wasn't messing around with the help?

"Gee, I can't imagine where they came from. . . ." Marga's face took on a perplexed—and no doubt, reflected Alex, what she considered to be sexy and helpless—expression. "Oh, now I remember!" Suddenly her confused air vanished. "I'm pretty sure they're Ed's. Maybe he left them in the car when I drove him to the airport."

Tired of what she was sure was a ridiculous charade, Alex feigned a yawn.

"We should be going," Vic said to Marga. "I'm sure our little crisis isn't of overwhelming interest to Alex."

Alex smiled at him, and after they'd left the casita she watched with dismay as the two of them stood talking by Marga's car. Finally they each entered their vehicles and drove off in opposite directions.

With a sigh, Alex turned and walked toward her empty bed.

A friendly ray of sunshine coming in between the curtains awakened her the next morning. A glance at her clock told her that it was eleven. She had slept an unbroken nine hours, a far cry from what she usually needed. The new job took more out of her than she realized, thought Alex, refusing to consider the possibility that her confused feelings about Vic made her mind seek out the peace of sleep. All she would think about now was how to lazily spend the day at her disposal. Suddenly she knew—she would try to get to the beach alone and meet Don and Jill there. Maybe the three of them could have dinner somewhere together.

She jumped up, showered and put on her most flattering bikini, a white one that showed both her tan and her figure to advantage. Knowing how small the American community was here, more than likely she'd run into Vic and Marga, and she was going to be ready. If war was declared, she'd fight with all her ammunition, and to the devil with Marga, who seemingly had no shame as far as conniving went. Marga would live to regret her manipulating ways, Alex swore to herself.

She caught herself. Why should she be antagonistic toward Marga, who had prior rights to Vic? Wasn't it natural that Marga should be jealous of her? After all, she'd certainly been hurt by the women Conrad had flaunted.

The sound of the jeep's motor interrupted her thoughts, and she was surprised to see it in front of her door. She might have guessed Vic would give her a lift today, since he probably knew from Don that she wouldn't get her car until Monday. His arrival was well timed. She had her beach bag ready.

"Didn't know if you wanted to check your gear and have breakfast on the boat." Vic's smile was warm as he greeted her. In the dazzling sunlight the sultry atmosphere of last night seemed no more real than a dream, thought Alex.

"Sure," she answered, walking to the jeep. "And frankly, I'm not sure if I went over my wet suit sufficiently yesterday."

She got in, and they drove down toward the pier. She tried to contain her excitement at being so close to him and had the feeling that Vic was going to ignore the night before, if the first occasion was any example. But this time she was driven to know what his real thoughts were. The rock steadiness of his muscular physique, the hard line of his jaw—did they only make her *think* he was not the type to play around? That he wasn't at all like Conrad? His words broke into her thoughts.

"Pepe will be out on the boat," Vic explained. "He knows how important this work is to me, and you must remember, he knows me from as far back as my undergraduate days, when I'd occasionally go out on his fishing boat when I was in this area working on digs. He's a man of tremendous dignity and great dedication."

Alex nodded, and silently added that the older Mexican had an innate sense of pride. She thought back to the time she'd offered Vic a different salary arrangement, and how that had offended his pride. But what about her own pride? she suddenly thought. She must know what Vic thought of Marga's little ploy the night before.

As if reading her mind, as he had seemed to do that morning when he arrived unexpectedly at the casita exactly when she was ready to leave, he changed the subject from Pepe to the preceding night.

"I must compliment you again on those photos," he told her. "They're invaluable."

Pleased as she was to hear his praise, she had to introduce the topic of Marga's arrival. "I'm glad to be of help," she replied, "though I'm sure I'd never be able to look after every little detail the way Marga does. Why, she couldn't even bear the thought of your going to bed without field glasses, even if they didn't belong to you."

She instantly hated herself for the cheapness of the remark. Though she felt she deserved the anger that would doubtless be his reply, her common sense was overcome by her need to know what this dark, often indecipherable man thought. He must realize that Marga's behavior was openly maneuvering.

To her surprise and embarrassment, however, her words sent him off into gales of laughter, his well-tanned skin crinkling at the corners of his eyes. Would she ever understand this man?

"Yeah, it was a sweet thing she did," was all he said. She burned inwardly, both at her own shame and with anger that he could not—or would not—see through Marga's schemes.

Mercifully they soon reached the pier where Pepe had drawn up the boat. As usual he was waiting on deck, and his eyes lit up to greet them. He welcomed them on board and walked them to the salon set with three places. Obviously Vic had been sure that she would come. Why hadn't she just told him to drop her off at Jill and Don's right away? She hated to see his ego boosted at her expense.

But when Pepe appeared with the meal, all her thoughts of staying away disappeared. She hadn't realized how hungry she was, until he placed before them a plate piled high with wheat cakes surrounded by little sausages.

"Thank God for a real breakfast," Vic exclaimed, serving first Alex and then Pepe, and finally loading his own plate with the golden cakes. "Bring on the maple syrup, Pepe!"

He turned to Alex. "I know this isn't the traditional

Mexican breakfast you may have expected," he informed her, "but usually on Sundays we Americans try to give ourselves an extra touch of home."

Just then Pepe appeared with a large tin of maple syrup, and she noted with delight that it was actually from Vermont.

"Could you expect anything less?" he joked with her, and she basked in the warmth of his smile. "I brought it down myself from Vermont, and I guard it with my life."

"Vermont?" she said, surprised. "You're from Vermont?"

"What's so strange about that?" he countered. "Why do you think I'm so interested in these southern climes?"

She had to laugh again, and could not help but appreciate his strong features, the broad shoulders which strained against his cotton shirt, his muscular arms. All of a sudden she pictured him in the bright plaid jacket and woolen hat of a lumberjack. It seemed so fitting that she could not stop herself from asking him if his family had ever been involved in the lumber business.

The laughter she'd gotten from him in the car was positively somber compared to the blast that greeted her most recent query.

"Lumber?" he repeated, his eyes filling with tears from so much laughter. "My father would love to hear that!"

She'd had enough of this man's mocking her. "What's so funny?" she demanded. "I thought it was a legitimate question."

"All right." He calmed down, but his eyes sparkled with amusement as he told her just why her question had struck him that way. "My father's president of the largest bank in Vermont," he told her, and here he reached out to touch her arm. The feel of his skin against hers almost burned her, and she wished he would never remove his hand. She fought to concentrate on his words. "My mother's family is into real estate, and two of my brothers have taken up careers in law. That leaves my sister, who's a doctor. My father's embarrassed that the three of them turned out so poorly—after all, he groomed all of us from day one for life in the bank—and you can imagine what he thinks of a son to whom sand-covered ruins are more important than the current interest rate. Oh, well," he concluded, a sense of sadness seeming to come over him, "maybe he would prefer lumber to what I'm doing now, but that's his problem, not mine."

They went on to finish the meal in silence, and Alex's respect for Vic and his dedication to his field grew. Obviously he could have had a very easy, ready-made life—if he'd been willing to give up what was important to him. Despite the wealth in his background, or perhaps because of it, he had the need to accomplish something on his own, to contribute to a body of knowledge to which he was drawn by love rather than by the desire for even more money. Here was another way in which he differed from Conrad.

The Bentleys welcomed Alex warmly when Vic dropped her off at their beautiful tile-roofed, adobe home. She would not allow herself to dwell on the fact that Vic was going to pick up Marga, and gave all her thoughts to Jill, who showed her around the gracious home. She gasped as they walked out onto a large patio, graced by tropical trees. "And you don't need the beach," she commented as she saw the flower-ringed pool, complete with lounging chairs and a corner bar.

"Oh, we enjoy the pool a lot," Jill said, "but on Sundays it's fun to go to the beach for a while. We'll come back here for dinner and drinks around the pool afterward."

"We love togetherness"—Don laughed—"but we try not to get too ingrown!" He hugged his wife, and both their faces glowed with happiness. For the second time that day Alex thought of Conrad, and quietly resolved that no one would ever hurt her that way again.

They changed and left for the beach, where they staked out their territory on the white sands. Slipping off her beach robe, Alex ran into the water for a long swim, enjoying her holiday. Fifteen minutes later she waded to shore and walked toward the Bentleys, who were sunning themselves on two big rattan mats. It wasn't until she was almost level with them that she noticed Marga and Vic, recently arrived, arranged on their own mats nearby. Marga was stretched out, face down, her suit straps slipped off her shoulders. A large and fashionable straw hat covered the back of her head. Alex saw Vic watching her progress over the sand, and she was glad she had worn her favorite bikini.

"Hi, Alex," he greeted her, and his eyes moved caressingly over her body, as they had the night before.

Was he so bold only because Marga had not yet lifted her head to acknowledge Alex's arrival? She wanted to ignore him but could not take her eyes from his long, lithe body, which seemed especially dark when contrasted with that of Don, who was office-bound most of the week.

She returned his greeting, and he continued to stare at her, making her feel self-conscious in the skimpy suit, something that had never happened on the California beaches, filled with body-builders.

Marga stirred and muttered something to her as the Bentleys lazily acknowledged her return. Waving casually in their direction, Alex stretched out on her towel and tried to soak up the sun with the rest of them, pulling a large-brimmed Acapulco straw hat over her eyes.

The waves gently lapped the shore, while farther out white sails moved slowly. Nearby, cries of the children running on the sand blended to make a joyful sound. Some teenagers began strumming a guitar and started to sing in harmony about unrequited love. Alex, lulled between sleeping and waking, was aware of a glowing sense of well-being that crept over her. She was filled with a calm and a happiness that she hadn't felt for a long time. It was an ideal Sunday, a perfect day, and even Marga's nearness failed to bother her. Soothed by the heat, almost hypnotized by the rhythmic sound of the waves against the shore, she felt herself drifting off to sleep.

Suddenly she sat up as the air was rent with shouts, screams and the sound of a speedboat approaching one of the nearby piers. Then she saw another, and another, finally counting five in all, each filled with boys yelling rodeo-style. Every boat headed straight for the pier, turning away only at the last possible moment. A hair-raising show, it was accompanied by enough noise to silence everyone on the beach. Children were open-mouthed, and sunbathers stood up abruptly. Vic leaped up like a shot and ran to the water, helping to get frightened, crying children back to safety. Though the teenagers were not about to drive their boats directly into the bathers' midst, noted Alex, the children were so terrified by the commotion that some of them might panic and drown. Don rose and followed Vic's lead.

Alex turned to Jill. "What in the world's going on?" she asked.

"It's the students," Jill wearily explained. "I thought that maybe this year they'd leave us in peace, but I was wrong."

"What students?" Alex wasn't aware of any university remotely near San Pablo.

"It's mid-term," Jill continued, "and some of the college kids meet in Tierra Quemada every year. It's another spot like Fort Lauderdale."

"Where the boys meet the girls?"

"That's it. And where the locals reach the end of their ropes!"

The women watched the scene in silence for a moment, and finally calm returned to the beach as the boats disappeared down the shoreline. At last Vic and Don were able to make their way back to them.

"Well, guess that does it for the beach today." Jill began to collect her paraphernalia. "Let's get out of here. Vic—Marga, come on over to our house. We've got a good dinner. Alex, I took it for granted you'd come."

They began to collect their things, Vic and Marga making sounds of grateful acceptance. Alex wondered how Marga would act toward her since last night's escapade, but she herself had resolved to be circumspect. Of course, in inviting them all, Jill and Don were unaware of any possible tension among the three of them, but Alex determined not to let anything change or spoil her Sunday. She didn't have to wait long for Marga's move. On the way to the cars, she suddenly found Marga walking beside her.

"Wasn't that silly of me last night?" Marga said, catching Alex's arm and giving her a forced smile. "I'm so busy and uptight with my job that I just can't remember everything—I could have sworn those glasses belonged to Vic."

Sure, thought Alex, but out of a desire not to make a scene, she decided to humor Marga—for now. "Let's forget it," Alex answered, deliberately waiting for Don and Jill to catch up with her. She watched as Marga was forced to move ahead, and against her will had to admire the other woman's almost sculpted figure, revealed by her open beach-robe. Could she truly compete with the dark-haired beauty, even supposing Marga didn't have an understanding with Vic? Though she herself had often been complimented on her wholesome good looks, wouldn't most men prefer a sultry woman like Marga? She bit her lip in self-doubt. Conrad had certainly taken away a lot of her confidence—would Vic do the same?

She pushed these thoughts to the back of her mind as they gathered in the patio by the Bentleys' pool to be served a typical New England dinner, which Jill had produced with her maid's help.

"Mmmm, this is the way I like it," Vic commented as he tasted the turkey dressing. "I just love this stale-bread stuffing. I almost feel as if I were back home."

Alex, noting that Jill colored with pleasure at Vic's praise, added, "I know what you mean. Just about everyone gilds the lily on stuffing when they want the simplest and best kind."

"I'll make you some, darling." Marga turned to Vic, patting his cheek. "Just be a little patient."

Right, thought Alex. Patient enough to let her learn what a kitchen was, and then just a little while longer till she could tell the sink from the stove! Her own cattiness surprised Alex. Wasn't her reaction just sour grapes? After all, she herself hated to have her professional skill doubted just because she was attractive. Marga's having the sculpted cheekbones of a high fashion model and always being elegantly dressed didn't mean she was as lost in the kitchen as she was when it came to remembering who had left things in her car. Despite these thoughts, however, her opinion of Marga's culinary prowess was confirmed when the other woman turned to Jill and asked in a voice full of syrupy concern, "Could you write the recipe down for me? I'm really a very good cook, but I never have the time."

Alex and Jill exchanged a quick, knowing look—any cook worth her salt would have such a basic recipe in the simplest of cookbooks at home. "Gee," responded Jill, "you know, I don't even use a recipe. This is just something I learned in my mother's kitchen—but then, I guess not all girls spend much time there. And being such a good cook, you probably do all sorts of complicated things. I can't tell if you'd enjoy such simple stuff, but I'd be more than glad to show you."

If Jill's meaning was lost on the two men, it certainly wasn't on Marga, for, Alex saw, she quickly changed the subject, asking Vic what he thought about the "just simply horrifying" show the students had put on at the beach that day. "It was such a good thing you were there, too," she cooed. "The scene on the beach would just have been chaos otherwise."

Though Alex for once agreed with her, she thought that the remark was not very considerate of Don, who didn't have the leadership quality that came so naturally to Vic. But her attention was quickly drawn from her own thoughts when Vic started to speak.

"Those students have no concern for the welfare of others—physical or otherwise," he began, his face so serious that it startled Alex. She'd never seen him this way. He'd been angry at times, especially when she'd first met him, she remembered with a grimace, but there was a different quality present now. "Their performance today made me realize just how little time I have to get on with my work, before these gold- and galleon-crazy boys make real problems." Neither Jill nor Don questioned him, knowing only that he was involved in an undersea project important to him.

He was right, thought Alex with a shock. The inquisitive students would be sure to think that Vic had discovered conquistadors' wealth or even pirate booty. She marveled that he hadn't mentioned these thoughts till now, though in retrospect she realized that they must have been among the first things to occur to him when the students started terrorizing the bathers. She felt proud that he'd made light of his own problems, then caught herself up sharply. He didn't belong to her; he belonged to Marga—and she was just wasting her time thinking about him. She quickly chastised herself. She was down here partly to forget an unpleasant experience with a man, not get hurt again. Or was it already too late? she reflected with fear.

She forced herself to return to the conversation. "Is there anything we can do?" she asked. "Maybe have Pepe keep the boat at a real distance from where we're diving . . ." Her voice trailed off. With all the work they had to do, their air supply barely provided enough time. If they had to travel any distance underwater before reaching the city, they'd have almost no time to accomplish anything.

He shrugged. "I don't know. But then"—he turned to Jill and Don—"those boys made enough trouble for us on the beach—let's not allow them to ruin a beautiful evening."

After dinner they moved to the poolside, and then Alex and Vic paired for a game of water polo against the Bentleys. Marga languished on the sidelines in a luxurious chaise longue, a tall ice-filled glass in her hand, having begged off from the game.

Again Alex was filled with confusion. When Vic brushed up against her, or even when he congratulated her on a good play, a sense of excitement coursed through her body. And Marga and her catlike eyes were only a few feet away! It was with relief that she greeted Jill's request to end the game, all of the participants almost out of breath by this time. By ten o'clock, when the Bentleys dropped her off in front of the casita, she wanted to forget everything on her mind—Vic, Marga, and now the threat the students posed to their very work.

As she walked toward the door, Don called out, "Oh, by the way—I've been able to rent a car for you, Alex. You won't be at our mercy any longer. It should be here by the time you return from the boat tomorrow."

"Thanks," she called out, and watched for a moment as the red Jaguar drove away down the tiny dirt road. It was a good thing she'd thought to speak with Don about getting a car, since Vic obviously wanted her to depend on him. Tired and still not sure of her feelings for him, she became suddenly bitter. Why, he'd probabably dangled a not-too-subtle offer of marriage before Marga to keep her in line, as much as such a thing was possible, and then figured he'd have Alex at his beck and call when Marga wasn't there.

Fatigued, she let herself into the little house, and for a reason she couldn't understand, burst into tears.

CHAPTER SIX

THE DIVE WENT well the next day. Alex took shots of everything Vic pointed out, although at times it seemed she was only photographing insignificant mounds, which were hard to distinguish from the natural ridges and rocks she had encountered many times on the ocean floor. Then, later, he took her farther into the ruins than she'd been before. She saw a silent, beautifully encrusted city, formations that bore mute testimony to an earlier grandeur. She longed to exclaim over its beauty, to communicate with him by voice—an impossible task in their wet suits. She signaled with her camera-laden arms flung out and she knew he understood. Slowly, both aware of an almost sacred atmosphere, they wandered in and out of coral-covered ruins, Vic pointing to what he wanted Alex to capture with her camera. It was a wrench to have to surface again, but she was adamant about not overstaying their alloted time on the bottom.

When they ascended and changed for lunch, they found that Pepe had outdone himself again. They heard him humming in the galley, and the fragrance of frying chicken floated into the salon. The table was quickly set, and they hungrily began their meal, realizing more than ever the energy diving demanded of them.

"The only cloud on the horizon is those damn students," Vic said between mouthfuls. "And to think in my own undergraduate days, I was probably right in the middle of a bunch like that, and one of the rowdiest."

"Everybody should have some wild young days!" Pepe declared. "If you don't take them while you are young, something terrible happens later on in life."

"Nothing worse than sowing wild oats past forty?" Vic asked, laughing.

"That's right!" Pepe replied seriously. "It's indecent. You see it every day—my uncle did it. Grew up in a decent, correct family. Went to mass every Sunday, because he was an altar boy. Even thought of studying to be a priest. Then married and had a nice family. But—when he reached fifty he fell in love with a pretty girl half his age, who had fallen in love with his money—he had a good business. And instead of just quietly keeping her as as his mistress—he left his family! Can you imagine—just turned *loco!*"

"And all because he didn't have his fling when he was young?" Alex asked.

"Of course that was it," Pepe replied. "What else? He wasn't a complete man when he married—then, nose to the grindstone—work, work, work. Then, along comes this pretty girl . . ."

"Did you have your wild days, Pepe?" Vic joked.

"Me? *Claro que sí.*" He smiled at him meaningfully. "Like I hear you say, 'you bet your life.' You don't know me!"

"Maybe that's why Pepe's so dependable now," Alex commented.

"Exactly, Señorita," he agreed. "And remember what I'm telling you, when it's time for you to get married again."

"Pepe, I wouldn't make a move without your advice"—she laughed—"but I'll tell you now, that'll be a long, long time away."

"There's a saying in Spanish." He smiled. "Man proposes, God disposes."

"That comes in English, too," Vic said.

"But you know those students and me," Pepe continued. "We were drinking beer together last night in Tierra Quemada."

"What?" Vic stopped eating to stare at him. "How in the world did you run into them?"

"Run into them? I asked them to meet me there," Pepe replied, placidly continuing to eat his lunch. "I heard they were planning to visit us here on the boat to see about diving with us."

"Oh, my God—just what I was afraid of!" Vic moaned. Alex wanted to put a hand on his arm to comfort him but didn't dare, as his face grew angrier and his body tensed visibly.

"My oldest son told me that they think we're diving for gold," Pepe continued.

"What did you tell them, Pepe?" Vic asked anxiously.

"Why, I invited them all to my house tonight for supper, of course!"

"Of course!" Vic exploded.

"It was the only thing to do," Pepe replied, still unperturbed.

What in the world was he doing? thought Alex.

A shocked silence held for a moment before he continued. "I thought I'd explain to them what's down there."

"Have you gone out of your mind, Pepe?" Vic demanded. "I told you that we've got to keep the whole thing secret until I'm ready to tell the scientific community."

"Calma, calma," Pepe soothed. "Don't get upset. You don't have to worry about anything. Many times I've handled situations like this. Plenty of people have tried to invade my fishing grounds, and I had to deal with them. Trust an old hand like Pepe."

"But Pepe—this is different!" Vic explained. "This involves—"

"Not another word, Vic." Pepe smiled, rising to clear the table. "Just you and the señorita be at my house about eight this evening—and of course bring your American friends."

Vic simmered down as Pepe left the room, but shot a questioning look at Alex, who was beginning to laugh.

"He's got something up his sleeve, can't you see? You can read it a mile away. He wants to surprise us, and he'll never tell you what it's all about. I'm going to be there, wherever his house is. I'll have my car today." She found her spirits soaring, pleased that the arrogant Vic had to worry, for a change.

"I don't think we'll continue in this spot this afternoon," Vic said, frowning. "Those kids will have slept off their hangovers and might be out in those speedboats watching. We'll chug along to an entirely different location."

"A good idea," she agreed.

"I can show you one of the most beautiful underwater landscapes in the world," he continued, still subdued. "I meant to tell you about it earlier, because you might get some good shots of it for one of the travel or photography magazines."

"Great!" she said, secretly pleased that the thought had crossed his mind.

"We can kill two birds with one stone," he said. "It's about half an hour away, and by the time we get into the water, we will have digested lunch."

They began gliding slowly by the shoreline in the direction of Tierra Quemada in order to attract the attention of the students. They picked up two speedboats, which began to follow them.

"Perfect," Vic said as he gazed out into the hazy distance. "Let them catch up with us, Pepe." He gave a friendly wave to the occupants, who waved back happily. They followed at a short distance and finally pulled up alongside the *Vera*. Vic allowed the four of them to board.

"We heard about you," they told him enthusiastically, and Alex noted they gave her some appraising looks. "The moment we hit town we heard all about the sunken ship. Located anything yet?"

"Not a thing in that line," Vic replied as Pepe hovered anxiously in the background. "What we really want are some good underwater landscape shots for a magazine. Ms. Wood, here, is getting ready to dive with her cameras now. Care to join us?"

"Oh, really, now—" The jean-clad, open-shirted leader laughed. "Don't pull that one on us! You're diving for treasure and don't want to say. Let us in on some of the fun, man. We don't want the bread, necessarily, only the fun of diving for a sunken ship. Just like we're going into Merida next Sunday, and Frank, here, is going to jump in the bull ring!"

"And maybe get killed?" Vic commented. "That is, if they don't catch him first and throw him in jail."

"Well, Frank, you'd better think that over, but man, what about letting us dive with you? This guy here said we could." He indicated Pepe. "Said he was going to explain the layout to us tonight."

"Sure, you can dive with us." Alex spoke up, trusting in Pepe. "Just get some wet suits ready for tomorrow." She looked at Pepe, refusing to let Vic catch her eye. Let him suffer for a bit.

As the boys returned to their boats, Vic shook his head wonderingly. "This better be good tonight, Pepe," he warned, though the tone of his voice told them he wasn't expecting to be pleased.

An hour later Vic led Alex down into the depths of another kind of wonderland, this one different from the sleeping Mayan city. She now felt happily free to shoot what she wanted. Inquisitive fish nudged against her—fish she had never seen before. Then she looked up from the white sandy bottom to see a school of the dangerous lion fish, which she caught by camera at a safe distance, signaling to Vic to stay away by giving him the sign for danger. A moray eel passed by, minding its own business, and they both kept their distance, aware of its venomous, tenacious bite if frightened or cornered.

But the most thrilling aspect of the scene was the

ridge of red coral which symmetrically bordered the site. Careful not to scrape along it and tear her wet suit, Alex took shot after shot of the stunning natural wall. As the depth was only half that of their regular dive, there was more light than she had been accustomed to, and she could better appreciate the blue-green seascape which seemed to extend for miles around them. It was tempting to stay below, and at the shallower depth she permitted more bottom time, but finally Alex had to give the signal to surface.

She could not contain her excitement once they were on board. "It's a real fairyland. Earth people don't know what they're missing," she exclaimed the moment they removed their face plates. "Thank you for showing to to me!"

Vic caught her excitement and told her more than she'd previously known about his discovery of the secret city. "It's unworldly, isn't it?" he agreed. "In fact, I've been fascinated by this place for a long time. Pepe knew of my interest in the area, and one day—and this was before I was even in grad school, remember—he told me that there was an old legend of a lost settlement in that area. I became obsessed by the thought of finding it someday. I'd read about Thompson's exploits as well, and so I did just about all of my graduate work on the Mayans."

Alex, who knew more about the salvaging and shooting of ruins once they were already located, was intrigued. "How did you find the actual city, though?" she asked. "I hate to use a hackneyed phrase, but it would seem harder to locate a city lost underwater for centuries than to find a needle in a haystack."

"It certainly is," he agreed, and again she could not help but admire the sense of determination and purpose he projected. "As an archeologist, of course I studied a great deal of geology. I combined what I knew of the recent—and by that I mean the past several millenia—geological history of this area with what archeologists before me had learned about the Mayans. Even then I could hardly believe that I was lucky enough to locate the city with only about a year's worth of actual looking out here."

He certainly was lucky as well as talented, thought Alex, remembering how long other archeologists with whom she'd worked had struggled, often in vain. But then, he also downplayed his skill. "That's fantastic," she commented, "but I'm so amazed by the beauty of both places—the city, and this coral."

His eyes met hers. "Yes," he agreed, "I can hardly tear myself away from here after a dive—especially one with an added attraction." Again he took in the length of her body, and she refused to falter under his gaze. Maybe he'd be even happier if he could convince Marga to get her hair wet and go under with him.

She thought suddenly that she'd like to return the following Sunday. Then she wouldn't have to endure Marga all day. She wondered if Pepe would bring her out in the boat. Or she could probably even rent her own, though she'd really prefer to have another diver along, not wanting to break a basic safety rule.

When she got home, she was pleased to find a car with keys in it in front of the house. A spunky little sedan with heavy tires, it would do well on the sharp gravel, occasional dirt roads and sudden hills of this part of the country. She tried it out, up and down the sea road in front, noting its excellent response and sturdy build. Don had chosen it well. She was independent and could drive where she wanted without relying on Vic. Perhaps now Marga would be less cutting toward her, too. But that evening Vic still honked for her at the dinner hour, calling out that Ed would be back, and that he would be expecting them to "rally round the flag." So she followed him into town, and they went to their usual table at the Taquito, where, as she had suspected they would be, all were gathered, with drinks.

"Welcome! Welcome! Welcome!" Vic greeted Ed, who rose. They gave the *abrazo,* much to Alex's surprise.

Ed turned to her. "Aren't you going to give me the abrazo?" he asked, feigning hurt and surprise.

"But you were only gone for a short weekend," she half protested.

"My dear girl! Don't you know we live in Mexico now? Don't give me that cold gringo attitude!"

They laughed as she submitted to the stylized handshake, hug on one side, and handshake again—the abrazo which seemed so indispensable to the warm Mexican way.

When she turned, Alex noted that, as usual, Vic and Marga sat together, just a little removed from the rest. Her attention was diverted by Don, who anxiously asked how she liked the car he had selected for her. Then Vic captured the interest of the group. Without mentioning his archeological finds, he spoke of his problem with the students and told them of Pepe's mysterious invitation at eight.

"I wouldn't miss it for the world," Jill exclaimed, seconded as usual by Don.

"Just what I need after sweating over a hot factory," Ed said facetiously. "Can I come, too?"

"Of course," Vic said. "I need all the help I can get. God only knows what Pepe's going to pull tonight! You're coming too?" he asked of Marga, who had remained passive during the excitement.

"Why, if you wish," she responded in a cool voice. Alex scoffed. Everyone knew there was absolutely nothing else going on in San Pablo.

They finished their drinks, keeping an eye on the time. Shortly, Vic rose. "Let's pay the check and get out of here. It's a ten-minute ride to Pepe's house, I think. Yes. He and his wife invited me there only once. You know very well that people like Pepe keep their homes sort of sacred from us."

"Sacred?"

"Just about," Vic said as he paid the waiter. "They don't want you immoral people with an entirely different culture to contaminate their kids. You didn't know that? I'll explain later, but right now, let's go!"

Marga and Vic left together, as did Don and Jill. Alex followed the caravan in her car, reveling in her new independence, declining Ed's invitation to ride with him. She eagerly anticipated the evening ahead. Whatever Pepe had up his sleeve, she wouldn't miss it for the world.

CHAPTER SEVEN

THEY ARRIVED AT a garden-fronted house with lights swinging in the back patio. Guitars were strumming as two or three dancing couples tried to find a disco beat in the music. At the door, Pepe's wife, an attractive woman who looked thirty-five, greeted them cordially, and they were all duly introduced to six children of varying ages, the oldest of whom was nineteen. Each impeccably dressed child greeted the guests with a solemn and formal handshake.

A chorus of wolf whistles from the college boys sounded as Alex, Marga and Jill entered. They were immediately surrounded and bombarded with questions and conversation in English. Alex saw the men relegated to the background, where they were plied with food and drink in the tradition of Mexican hospitality. Pepe and his wife did the same for them, almost immediately pressing *Cùba libres* into their hands.

As the groups shifted, formed and shifted again, Alex found herself in a circle which included Vic, who at one point cornered Pepe.

"What the heck is this all about, Pepe?" she heard him ask in Spanish.

"All in good time." Pepe smiled back, giving a wink which included her too. "All I ask of you, Vic, is to translate for me as I go along—okay?"

"Translate—for what?"

"All in good time—you'll see," came the answer as he left them.

Ed drifted up to them, trailed by Marga, who, Alex could see, was fully enjoying the special attention the boys were giving her.

"They're terrific hosts down here," Ed commented as one of the children took his empty glass for a refill. "They never want anyone to be *triste*—sad, that is. Always seeing you have plenty of attention."

"That's what spoils people who come here and mix with the nationals," Don replied. "Get back to the States, and at any party you're on your own!"

"A great group of fellows here," Marga declared. "I've had a scad of invitations to dance. But I thought I'd let you have the first one." She turned to Vic, smiling, and took his arm.

Alex turned away, only to be quickly claimed by one of the students. She strained to hear Vic's voice, which at that moment laughingly encouraged Marga to go ahead and have a good time with the kids. Alex thought to herself that they seemed to understand each other perfectly, and forced herself to pay attention to the enthusiastic twenty-year-old who was chattering away to her. He ended by pulling her out to dance.

"Love that beat!" he shouted over the din. "We made the son of the house put on some of *his* records. Guitars are fine for mood music, but for dancin'—give me disco!"

Alex fell in with his spirit, laughingly gyrating to the music with him, trying to make herself enjoy the evening without worrying about either Vic or Marga.

The record stopped at last, and immediately the air was filled with a raucous, demanding music containing mostly brass. In marched a group of eight mariachis, dressed in authentic costumes. Silver buttons ran the length of their tapered striped pants, there were more silver buttons on their braid-decorated jackets, and each musician wore a large traditional Mexican sombrero. All conversation halted as everyone delightedly turned to watch and listen.

"Pepe didn't spare the horses," Alex heard Vic shout to Ed, who was beside him. "Mariachis don't come cheap!"

A half hour of music followed, and slowly the mariachis filed out, still playing. The party seemed to have reached its peak. As Alex stood in a group including Vic, Ed, Don and Jill, a student she recognized as one of their visitors on the boat that morning came over to them.

"I got to tell you, man," he said to Vic, "this is the greatest! I haven't had so much fun since the end of last exam period. We sure appreciate this a lot!"

"Better than swigging beer every night in some lousy joint!" another added as he sauntered up. "And the women here! Every living one could be a movie star—gosh, they're pretty!" He flashed what he obviously thought was a devastating smile at Alex, who struggled not to laugh.

"Oh, it's nothing at all," Vic replied, smiling broadly now himself. "We do this all the time—don't we?" He turned to Alex, who quickly nodded in assent. It was one of the few remarks he had addressed directly to her all evening.

"Yipee! *Viva México!*" a third student shouted, and

soon they began their college cheer, substituting "México" for the name of their midwestern alma mater.

Alex saw Pepe move to the center of the crowd, and her sense of excitement grew. Whatever he had in mind would be starting soon.

"And now, ladies and gentlemen"—Pepe raised his voice authoritatively—"would all the potential divers follow me into the house? Señor Victor and I are going to explain our program, and we'll see a couple of reels of home movies to illustrate."

"This is super!"

"Now comes the nitty gritty!"

"The crunch! We can swank back at school. I bet it's the sunken ship!"

As Alex heard them comment, following the crowd into the small front room, she began to feel her first misgivings. Pepe seemed confident, but how could he protect Vic's find, yet lead these boys on like this? The room was now darkened, and a white sheet was hung up in place of a movie screen. Gradually the murmuring ceased as Pepe took his place on one side and motioned to Vic to take his on the other side. The oldest son was threading an ancient projector.

"As you know, my boss, here, Señor Victor Clarke, is a scientist, who wants to do something for humanity." Pepe began turning to Vic to translate. Vic, Alex noted, conquered an initial quaver before repeating the English version. Yet it seemed to her that he had decided to play it straight, remaining serious.

"We dive, and sometimes we do find interesting things at bottom—at least *they* do," Pepe continued.

"But our main purpose is to experiment with the shark repellents which the señor has concocted. Something new, it's entirely different from what they sell now. I hope you boys will keep this secret—especially if you do participate."

A murmur went through the group as Pepe paused. Alex was glad the room was darkened, so her amazement wouldn't show.

"The only way to test the stuff is to try it on live sharks in their own ocean water, of course."

Vic now seemed more involved in his role, and a new tone came into his voice as Alex noticed him adding occasional flourishes of American idioms to his translation.

"It happens that I have more than a little experience with sharks," Pepe continued, still serious, "and I can usually locate their areas, their feeding grounds. Now, I don't want to say that San Pablo or Tierra Quemada is a dangerous place to swim—people are perfectly safe. But we go to the far areas, where I can locate them, where for years I have known them to gather. That's our mission. I find the sharks, and Señorita Alex and Señor Victor go down and try their repellents. Now let me show you how I began with the sharks. José, run the film!"

The screen lit up, and a fuzzy, out-of-focus picture showed; it soon cleared, and to the amazement of everyone, a younger Pepe was being pulled along, clinging to the tail of a thrashing white shark. Sometimes man and fish disappeared from the picture, only to appear again, traveling in the opposite direction. Now there was Pepe climbing on the back of the fast-swimming animal, then slipping down its sides. Then another swimmer came up to catch the tail. Pepe regained his balance, and then all went under when the fish plunged. The foamy water alone showed a moment. The film itself slowed and finally stopped as José quickly adjusted the sprockets of the old machine. When the picture continued, Pepe appeared with a group pulling the shark onto the beach, all of them mugging frequently at the camera. Then came a close-up of the shark with its gasping open mouth, showing nightmare teeth dripping sea water.

The ugly, thrashing death was shown in all its agony; then, strung up, at peace at last, the shark was shown surrounded by sunburned laughing boys, of whom Pepe was the foremost. The projector shuddered, then slowed to a stop. Everyone in the room was silent.

"Jaws!" someone exclaimed.

Alex, intrigued, wondered what would come next.

"Now, those were the days of my youth," Pepe continued, with Vic still translating, "and these brave people here are taking up the challenge. I do admit, I *was* a little careless once and almost got my leg bitten off. My wife won't let me show the scars any more, otherwise—"

A hubbub drowned him out as the lights went on. Alex watched as Pepe was deluged with questions coming from all sides, questions he was eager to answer. At last he pointed to the walls, hung with various framed pictures few had bothered to notice before. Alex noted that each of them showed him recklessly riding a shark while grinning at the camera.

"Now, anyone wanting to help us out in the name

of science, please be ready tomorrow morning," Pepe concluded as he modestly removed himself from center stage.

It was all Alex could do to keep from laughing out loud, but she could see that Don and Jill, nearby were nonplussed. Ed, behind her, seemed furious.

"My God—you're risking your life!" he exploded at Vic, whom Alex had watched making his way through the crowd toward them.

She was pleased to see Vic playing his role to the hilt. After the tension of not knowing what Pepe had had in mind, he had obviously decided to have a good time.

"Ed," he explained, "everybody has his own dream. If I can contribute to science this way, far be it from me to ignore the challenge."

Alex turned away to suppress a rising giggle. She wanted to laugh loudly and also to reassure them, but how could she interfere at this point?

"Oh, shut up, Vic," Ed snorted. "Spare me the histrionics. What about Alex, here? Is it fair to risk her life?"

"Don't you let her get into those shark's teeth!" A concerned student approached Vic.

Marga came up to them, alarmed. "Darling!" She reached for Vic's hand. "Please, for my sake, stop this business. It's madness—it's . . . *dangerous!*"

Alex suppressed a pang of jealousy that cut into her humor as she listened to Marga's determined pleas. Another student approached them. "Now tell me the truth—is that really the size of it? *That*'s your program?" he demanded.

"Well, actually, it isn't as dangerous as it looks—

or sounds," Vic invented. "You see, nine times out of ten the new repellent works!"

"But man, what about that *tenth* time!" came a yelp.

"Well, the averages are better than in Russian roulette, anyway." Vic shrugged, breaking away to look at the pictures, with Marga following closely behind him.

Ed took Alex by the arm and bore her to the patio, which was now relatively quiet. "I think you're foolhardy, young lady," he began as they sat on one of the benches. "Unless you tell me it's not true. Is this a come-on to get rid of the kids, or something?"

"Or something," she admitted, accepting a drink from one of the children. "Please don't worry. Pepe will explain everything later—or Vic will. And to think Vic and I didn't think he could swim! He's got a lot of explaining to do!"

After an ample supper, the party ended gradually, with Pepe giving the signal for the final song. "Enough! Enough!" He spread out his arms. "I'm a good Mexican host, but we all have to have an early start tomorrow for the sharks. All shark-hunters meet on the deck of the *Vera* at seven."

Reluctant goodbyes were said, and the boys roared away toward Tierra Quemada in several cars, giving their adapted college cheer for Pepe and Mexico.

Ed gathered together Alex and the others to say good night to Pepe, now smiling wisely at them all.

"Pepe, you had us fooled all along!" Vic laughed, slapping him on the back. "And Alex and I thought you couldn't even swim!"

"I can swim, all right," Pepe replied. "I just don't

plan to do any diving in those crazy suits! It's dangerous!"

"And pray tell, what do you call shark-riding?" Ed demanded.

Alex could no longer hold in her laughter. It rippled up infectiously, making Pepe and Vic join in together, unable to control themselves.

Marga bristled. "I really don't see anything funny about it," she declared.

Jill looked at her a moment, then at the laughing trio. "Can't you see it's a put-on! It must be!"

"Of course it is," Don said, and he too began to join in. *"Jaws!"* Don imitated the boys' exclamation.

"What about that *tenth* time?" Vic imitated, beginning to laugh again.

Alex released her pent-up emotions and at the same time felt she was sharing something with Vic from which Marga, now almost angry, was excluded.

"Why wasn't I told before?" she demanded. "That's a heck of a joke to play!"

As Vic tried to explain that neither he nor Alex had known what Pepe was going to do, he helplessly broke down again. Finally they were able to stop.

"But I still don't understand," Ed told them. "I never heard of this fooling around with sharks."

"When I was young and crazy," Pepe explained, "I was a beach boy in Acapulco, with my own little boat to rent. Every so often an old rogue shark would get trapped in the bay, and we had a lot of fun with it before we caught it."

"But a shark is a shark! Those teeth!" Ed insisted.

"You just make sure to stay out of the way of the

teeth while you're having fun," Pepe continued. "But we all rode those sharks. I don't see what all the fuss is about—this picture, *Jaws*. If no blood's in the water and you can swim all right, you can do it. We had real fun in those days—almost twenty years ago. A nice tourist took those films and gave me a copy."

"But Pepe, you never go in the water now," Alex commented.

Pepe gave her a smile. "I'm a family man now, Señorita. It's only a small family of six, but still a family. Remember I told you the time to do those things, to have your fling, is when you're young. Believe me when I say I have had my fling!"

"And doubled in spades!" Ed told him. "I take it, then, that this little charade was to scare the kids away?"

"Of course," Pepe answered. "Not one will show up tomorrow morning. That moving picture did the work for us."

"And you did a real favor for me," Vic said, shaking hands with him. "We'll meet you at the pier tomorrow—that is, if I don't have a hangover—your fault for being such a great host."

"Could I meet you on the boat at lunchtime?" Alex asked Vic. "I want to develop the shots I took this afternoon."

Vic considered a moment. "All right. Lunch on the boat, and then we'll put in a full afternoon."

That matter resolved, Alex again turned her attention to Marga, who stood stiffly off to one side. Alex now knew that a few moments without being the center of things annoyed Marga, especially when she, Alex, had engaged in a few words with Vic. As they slowly made their way to the cars, accompanied by Pepe and his wife, she saw Marga's arm go up to Vic's shoulder, pulling him nearer. "You sure had me worried, darling," she said loudly enough to be heard by all. Alex could not hear Vic's reply.

They all stood for a moment by Ed's car and talked, but Alex noted that Vic pulled Pepe aside. She was able to hear him as he spoke.

"Pepe, you know you didn't have to go to all that expense to help me out. Those mariachis cost a fortune, and what with all that supper and the drinks—"

"I know I'm a poor man, Vic," Pepe interrupted, "but I don't live to work, I work to live, and every now and then we all have to let go—to enjoy ourselves. It's worth it!"

"But besides the expense—all the preparation—your time—" Vic protested.

"Ah, Vic, don't you know what they say down here? *Hay mas tiempo que vida!*"

"There's more time than life," Vic translated in English, slowly nodding. "But still—"

"Did you all enjoy yourselves?" Pepe demanded of the whole group.

"You bet we did!" they answered almost in unison. Alex saw that even Marga had unbent enough to join the chorus.

"Then the whole thing was worth every peso, plus getting rid of the college boys!" Pepe announced. "And now that Vic has the help of the señorita Alex," he continued with a broad smile in her direction, "everything will be smooth sailing from now on." As Ed,

Don and Jill murmured their assent, Alex caught Vic's eye and could tell he too was pleased. Then, however, Marga flashed her a look of rage, and Alex knew that smooth sailing was the last thing she could expect.

Despite her premonition, Alex was pleased to note that she and Vic spent a most productive week after Pepe's party. Everyone was glad to hear, she knew, that the college crowd suddenly decided to go into Merida to see a bullfight, leaving San Pablo and Tierra Quemada a little duller but more peaceful without their presence. The news that from there they would be heading to Mexico City to fly back north for their spring semester brought even more relief. Alex breathed easier, and even though Vic carried on as if he'd not given the students another thought, she knew him well enough by now to understand he too was calmer.

In fact, though all the Americans were busily involved with their own projects, Vic was now the most dynamic and enthusiastic when they met for dinner and English conversation at the Taquito. To Alex's delight, he told her he was so pleased with their pictures that he had decided to photograph the entire area. Now there were times when Alex forgot her former problems, so involved had she become with the completion of the dives and photographs of what she now called the Secret City. Working daily with Vic, she was able to observe what real dedication was. To this was added the real excitement of just being near him—a feeling she had never known with Conrad.

Now that Alex had her own car and was no longer dependent on Vic to chauffeur her around, Marga had Vic to herself without having to worry about any after-hours fraternizing between Vic and Alex. But Marga seemed less happy than ever. In addition, Alex noted the beginnings of another element in Marga's covert glances at her. They were now evaluating, suspicious, as if she sensed Alex's feelings for Vic. Both to thwart Marga and to avoid what could only be a disappointing involvement, Alex started to give more attention to both Ed and the Bentleys at dinner and when planning her own free time.

One night, after dinner in San Pablo, she realized just how successful she'd been in establishing friendships and showing Ed that she was an organized woman. The two of them sat at the table as the Bentleys and Vic and Marga danced. Though Marga was sending her self-satisfied looks, her arms draped possessively over Vic's strong body, Alex was determined to ignore them.

"I don't know how I have the nerve to ask you this," Ed said, so that her attention quickly turned back to him, "but I wonder if you can help me with something."

"Sure, Ed, what is it?" Her curiosity was piqued, and she was pleased to have something to take her mind off Marga and her cat-that-just-ate-the-canary expression.

"It seems that all the Pittsfield chiefs of the main plant are coming down to see what's happening here with my branch. I've got to entertain them personally, along with the Mexican executives, and frankly, I don't have the slightest idea of how to start. In Massachusetts, we'd usually go to Tanglewood, then back to my home for an old-fashioned American barbeque. But, as you know so well by now, Alex"—and here he rolled his eyes upward in mock despair—"this town has so few resources. Could you help me with some ideas?"

"Of course, Ed," she replied, her spirits soaring. But she knew she must ask the obvious question. "By the way, isn't Marga, your assistant, the logical person to arrange all this?"

"Well"—he leaned toward her and spoke in a conspiratorial tone—"Marga will be handling all the executive details, but I don't think she's very strong in the domestic line." Alex laughed, remembering Marga's remarks regarding her cooking skills when she'd asked Jill for the stuffing recipe. "In fact," Ed continued, "she invited us all over to her place when we first got here, and even with a maid, the food was awful. She always says she's a good cook and just doesn't have the time—but I'm sure all her talk is for the benefit of you-know-who."

Alex felt herself go suddenly pale underneath her tan. She fought to keep a smile on her face, to keep tears from filling her eyes at this reminder that Vic belonged to Marga and would never belong to her. Then she chastised herself, reminding herself that her attraction to Vic was nothing more than a silly infatuation. As soon as she left the soft nights and sun-graced days of Mexico, as soon as she could break away from the moon that cast a Mayan spell upon her, she wouldn't give him a second thought.

She was glad Ed continued to speak, for she knew she would not be able to hide the quaver in her voice.

"And one great favor," he was saying. "Do you think you could act as hostess—I don't mean that in any way *chueco*," he quickly assured her, using the

Spanish word for "crooked."

Alex nodded quickly in agreement, already enthused by the challenge—and by the idea of putting on a show that would leave no doubt in Vic's mind as to just how capable she was.

"I'd be happy to help," she said. "After they look over the operation and the books and personnel, you don't know what to do with them—is that it?"

"Right. These people come down here thinking every part of Mexico is like Guadalajara, Mexico City or Acapulco, and I can't get it into their heads that San Pablo is a village!"

"Leave it to me." She smiled. "We'll use what makes this place different—the beautiful ocean, good food, terrific landscapes and seascapes and plenty of big yachts to rent—plus your own house, which I hear is terrific—swimming pool and all."

"But will that be enough for them?"

"Ed—" she laughed, "you've had too much of San Pablo. It'll be all new to them." She grew more and more excited as she spoke. "We'll have a day on a yacht, with mariachis and a good dinner, and if anyone wants to scuba dive, I'll take them down to a white, sandy wonderworld. Then there's big-game fishing to be had—oh, lots of things."

Ed was visibly heartened. "I might have known you'd come to the rescue," he said, impulsively grabbing her hand.

"Just call me the calvary!" She laughed. "How long are they staying?"

"Just three or four days, then they go on to Mexico City."

"Well, Mexico City can be just like Paris, Rome

or Madrid, with its luxurious buildings and night spots. But we'll make them remember San Pablo for a long while."

"Okay. We've got a week. You can get together with Señora Davila, my housekeeper, and whatever you need or want, just work it out together."

"That'll be terrific," Alex said. "When can I go over your house to see the layout?"

"How about tomorrow after dinner?"

"Fine," she replied. "*Hasta mañana*, then. Now I'd really better get back home." She rose and, walking past the dance floor, couldn't help giving Marga a wide smile and a wave goodbye.

The next evening's conversation at the Taquito dwelt largely with the coming "invasion," as everyone called it. Don and Jill talked shop with Ed, joined frequently by Marga, who now exhibited her professional know-how. The first such inspection since the inauguration of *Fâbrica Hierro-Acero*, it presented quite a challenge.

"There's really no need to get uptight about things," Don assured Ed. "All departments are working well. It's just that from the moment we broke ground for the building, everything has taken twice as long to complete as we planned."

"That's often the case in foreign countries," Ed replied, "and I think the main office is aware of it."

"But it's frustrating sometimes," Jill added. "By the way, shouldn't Don and I have a cocktail party, or something, for the men? Some of them are our personal friends anyway."

"Oh, sure! I need all the help I can get," Ed said. "Thank goodness Alex, here, is handling the social side. She's already got a yacht trip planned and some big-game fishing."

"Alex?" Marga repeated, her voice sounding somewhat strained. Alex knew she was struggling to keep a pleasant expression on her face.

"Yep," Ed replied, "'cause you, Marga, have a hell of a lot to do with the business coordination, just like Don and Jill. I hope to bring a fresh approach with Alex. She's agreed to think up some great Mexican entertainments—with Mrs. Davila's help, of course."

His praising her so highly in front of Marga worried Alex—well, too bad. Marga had Vic, so what was she complaining about?

"You might have checked with me," Marga replied. "I could have managed."

"Yes, and then you would have told me you were overworked again, right?" Ed shot back. "Vic, maybe I should've asked you first, but Alex says everything will be on her own time." He looked from Vic to Alex.

"To tell the truth," she said, "I don't think it will take much time, since it's easy to charter a yacht and hire mariachis. Ed and I are going over to his house tonight to make further plans with his housekeeper."

"Would anyone like to come along?" Ed invited. "We can continue our meeting there."

"Thanks a lot, but I'm dead," Jill declined. "Don can go if he likes."

"Rain check for me," Don said with a yawn. "Twenty-four hours of thinking about the *fábrica* is too much for even me."

"Vic and I are going for a ride on the shore road," Marga said with a significant glance at Alex. "I'm sure you two can manage perfectly well without us."

"Maybe better." Ed laughed and broadly winked at Alex. "I only invited you to be polite," he joked.

Though they all laughed, Alex detected a harsh look in Vic's eyes. But she didn't care if he was angry. The support she was giving Ed was not time-consuming, and her work on the dive was going very well.

Then a sudden thought struck her. Could he possibly think she was interested in Ed, who was thirty years her senior? Did he think she couldn't exist without someone to go around with?

Obviously Vic only saw her as someone upon whom to exercise his masculine charm. Yet she knew that her new independence freed her from his control, and she was sure that rankled. Well, she'd show him.

Watching Vic out of the corner of her eye, she said, "I'm really eager to see your house—I'm sure it'll help me get more ideas for the invasion."

Alex felt a perverse satisfaction at seeing Vic's expression visibly darken and his lips tighten. Oblivious to the change in him, Ed blithely invited him over for a nightcap later that night. Although Alex wanted to make Vic angry, she had no desire to confront him in Ed's house and was relieved when he tersely declined.

They parted soon after, and Alex followed Ed in her car along some secondary roads, to pull up in front of what was obviously a mansion. Spanish-style, it was rambling, beamed and indirectly lighted with a masterful touch. Light from an invisible source also made the grounds glow. Farther along she noticed a huge swimming pool, the green water lit from below.

"This is stunning—a sultan's palace!" Alex exclaimed as they began walking across the lawn.

"Thanks. Señora Davila keeps it all lit up for me until I get home—usually late."

They walked slowly past beautifully landscaped flower beds, shrubbery, trained vines and pink paving-stones surrounded by manicured grass.

"Oh, what a wasted spot," Alex commented. "You seem never to be home—you never entertain . . ."

"That's why I'm depending on you," he replied, guiding her through one of the entrances into the house. "I'm completely out of practice. And that darn *fábrica* takes all my time. I only relax when I'm with our group."

Alex drew in her breath as they entered a sunken living room, one of whose walls was a waterfall. Even at the home of Conrad's family she'd never seen anything as stunning. Again she was surprised that Marga didn't set her sights on Ed.

"Señora Davila knew we were coming and turned that on," Ed said. "She's got a sense of the dramatic."

"It'd be a waste if you didn't have a bash here," Alex said, sinking down into one of the mushroom-colored sofas. "How many of your colleagues have a waterfall in their living room?"

"Not many, I guess. This house was one of the few available to me in town. It's rented, of course. It was built by a famous Mexican architect, who stays in Europe most of the time." He was busy getting a margarita for her. "It just happened we were *simpático* with each other, as they say down here; we really got along. Otherwise he wouldn't have rented it to me. He's a real artist and doesn't give up his creations easily. I happened to meet him on the beach, and we got to talking. Presto—a comfortable would-be bachelor's pad."

"Would-be?" she asked, but before she could question him further, she heard someone enter the room.

It must be Señora Davila, she realized, turning to see a small woman. A brilliant smile lit up the woman's entire face, and she welcomed them in Spanish as though she were the chatelaine of the house, which indeed she must have felt herself to be. Alex thought she looked the part, with her simple black dress, jet-black ropes of beads, black shoes and stockings and her hospitable air.

"I tell the señor," she was saying, "he never brings anyone here—never gives a fiesta—never enjoys his home—never shows it off! And now he tells me that we can have a party. And you will help me with all the menus and tell me what these Yanquis will like to eat! Maybe a *barbacoa?*"

"Maybe," Alex agreed, "but we've got to have some other Mexican food. They think all the food down here is chili. Let's show them the four-thousand-year-old tradition of Mexican cuisine."

"Oh, of course! But when I said barbacoa, I meant the real Mexican barbacoa—underground cooking, with banana leaves covering everything, and consommé dripping in the pan underneath."

"Perfect!" Alex exclaimed.

"And we've got the apparatus right on these

grounds," the señora continued. "And the gardener, Chucho, knows just how to manage it."

They talked for about half an hour before an enthused Señora Davila left the room, only after inquiring, in the Mexican tradition, if she could offer them anything further.

"She's wonderful," Alex told Ed when they were again alone. "I see that between us you're going to be called the 'host with the most on the ball'!"

"I'll drink to that," Ed said, laughing.

Alex noticed that he seemed more carefree, and couldn't help but be amazed by the workings of a mind that could handle all sorts of business emergencies yet was thrown into a quandary when faced with planning three days' of entertainment for fewer than ten people.

Neither of them spoke for a minute, and then Ed returned to the topic that had been interrupted by Señora Davila's entrance.

"I should probably explain a few things to you," he said, settling into a chair, his drink in his hand. "This is, for all intents and purposes, a bachelor pad."

He paused, and when Alex did not comment, he continued, "I'm not going to tell you my wife doesn't understand me, or anything like that, because she understands me perfectly. And I understand her. It's just that we've each lived our own lives separately for the past fifteen years."

Here Alex quickly drew in her breath. Though she felt sorry for Ed, she immediately saw the major stumbling block to Marga's pursuing him for his money. But why hadn't Marga tried to maneuver him into a divorce? She certainly seemed capable of it—after all,

Ed thought she was sweet and overworked rather than calculating.

Ed seemed to sense what was going through her mind, or at least some of it. "For some reason, my wife's always refused me a divorce," he said, "and I'm not going to push the issue—I'm no kid and I'm not out to marry again. She's from one of the best families in Massachusetts, you know." His eyes met hers. "No divorce in it."

"I'm sorry," Alex said softly. She remained silent, pondering the problems that love could bring. Ed touched a button by his side, and music filled the room.

"That's my story, and if necessary I'll supply some handkerchiefs," he said, in a heavy attempt to lighten the moment. "Now, shall we see the rest of the house? I'm supposed to put up the president and the vice-president. Maybe you could suggest which rooms they should have." He rose and went over to take her empty glass.

"Gosh, I'm sorry, Ed. It must be tough to contend with that kind of situation," she said, rising. She took his hand in a sympathetic gesture, and they moved toward the stairs.

They turned abruptly, however, at the sound of a deep voice. Vic had just been shown into the room by Señora Davila.

"I thought I'd take you up on that nightcap you offered awhile ago," he said, and Alex detected a note of forced casualness in his tone.

Ed seemed to hesitate a moment, about to say something, then changed his mind. "Hello, Vic. You'll find the drinks in the bar, over there. I'm taking Alex up to see where the prexy and vice-prexy are going to sleep while here. We'll be down shortly—unless you want to come."

"Oh, no," he replied, going toward the bar. "I'll get my drink and wait."

As they checked the lavishly-appointed upstairs bedrooms, Alex suddenly turned to Ed. "I wonder why Vic decided to come after all. It's almost as if he's checking up on me, although he made it quite clear when he hired me that our lives were our own."

"I understand Vic perfectly," Ed said knowingly. "At the moment I think I know him better than he knows himself."

Alex frowned, puzzled. What did Ed mean? Vic still seemed angry with her. Had he really been trying to check up on her? Or was he getting cold feet about his engagement to Marga, which she was probably urging him to make official, now that their work was nearing completion? That state of affairs she herself had helped bring about, through her photographic skill, she reflected ruefully.

When they reentered the living room, Vic was sitting on the couch, waiting for them.

"All squared away?" he asked. "I hope so, since Alex has to be ready for diving at seven tomorrow morning. I don't have anything to do with her social life, as you know, but she *is* under contract."

Alex tensed. As if she had ever skirted her responsibilities! He probably just wanted to get her away from Ed.

Ed, meanwhile, had taken offense as well. "And

I could remind you," he said, "that Margà is under contract to the *fábrica* and you've kept her out until all hours upon occasion. Have I ever said anything to you about it? She's turned up late at the office several times."

Vic's face darkened. "Being late at the *fábrica* is a different situation from being physically fit for diving at seven in the morning."

"I don't see a bit of difference, Vic, and frankly, I don't appreciate your interference. I think the whole thing's up to Alex."

Alex, fascinated by this turn of events, felt obligated to smooth over the situation. "We've finished for the evening, in any case, Vic. I'm doing this on my own time, and you don't have to worry about me—being late, I mean. But we can go now."

"I'll see you both out, then," Ed said, raising his eyebrows. "Thanks a million, Alex. See you tomorrow about the rest of it."

Vic and Alex got into their separate cars in the driveway and left, Alex following the speeding jeep. Her anger grew as they drove. He had neither a reason nor the right to follow her to Ed's house. In the first place he was fully involved with Marga, and in the second place he had clearly laid down the ground rules of their relationship. Who had broken them? Vic—twice, with kisses which had sent her reeling.

A sharp turn made by Vic on two wheels of the jeep jerked her back to reality. She slowed to take the turn more gradually, and later easily shortened the distance between them. They were now approaching the shore road, which was wider.

The evening had filled her with confusion. What exactly had Ed meant when he said, "At the moment I think I know him better than he knows himself"? Was it at all possible Vic was fighting an attraction to her? She pondered the new question as they pulled up in front of her casita. Getting out, she waved at Vic, expecting him to continue up the road to his place. She was surprised to see him park and get out of the car.

"I just want a couple of words with you," he said, following her inside. "For your own sake."

"Oh?" she asked, feeling renewed anger welling up inside her. "Then come on in. But don't forget about seven tomorrow morning. It's almost midnight now."

She turned on her lights and sat down at the table, turning to look inquiringly at him.

"Look, Alex, I did say that our social lives would be separate, but I just want you to know that Ed is married!"

"I know that," she replied, though she wasn't about to let him know she had just discovered it.

She purposely had not asked him to sit down, but now he did so on his own. He was tense, but his anger only served to make him more attractive. He put a hand on her arm and said, "Look Alex, how can I make you understand? This nonsense about the 'invasion,' that he can't handle the social part—it's pure, unadulterated crap! He's looking for an excuse to get next to you." He slammed his other hand down on the table.

"Vic, you don't understand the relationship between me and Ed at all. And at any rate, may I ask what business it is of yours even if he were trying to 'get next to' me, as you put it?"

"It's just that I can't stand by and see you being taken advantage of like that. Ed's in his fifties and you're twenty-six. What he's doing is unfair to you!"

Alex attempted to control her anger. She had no desire to hear about Vic's so-called concern for her well-being.

"Listen, Vic, Ed is down here trying to get a big job off the ground. He's got a lot to do on the business side of these people's visit, and all he asked me to do was to give him some ideas about how to entertain them . . . got it? He's never made a pass at me, if that's what you're hinting about him. He's more like a father!"

"Yes, and I suppose that little trip to the bedrooms was a part of his way of getting your help to entertain his friends! If I hadn't come along, don't think for a moment you would have gotten down those steps—"

"Without meeting a fate worse than death?"

Now he was furious. "I'm serious, Alex! I'm only trying to take care of you. I'm responsible for you!"

"Oh, I wasn't aware of that," she said, surprised. "I thought that off the boat, 'I'm *me* and you're *you*.' Your words, I think."

"You're impossible, Alex. Have it your own way, then. You told me you've just been divorced. Sometimes people like you get involved on the rebound, don't forget. A disastrous rebound! That's why I spoke."

"Thanks a lot for your concern, Vic. Don't think

I don't appreciate it—really, I do. But up to now, I've been able to deal with wolves—I've had my share in my time. And as for that fate worse than death—I was taught self-defense at an early age."

"Got all the answers, haven't you?" He glared at her.

"And some of the questions," she riposted.

"Then I'll butt out!"

"I'll thank you for it."

He jumped up and walked to the door. She followed slowly to shut and lock it. "I'll be at the pier at seven," she said. "Try to get a good night's sleep, Vic," she told him wearily, tired of the misunderstandings, of having to hide her feelings. "Things will look different in the morning."

He turned suddenly and came inside again, shutting the door behind him. Catching her arm, he pulled her to him. "Alex!" he said. "Alex! You—you're a devil! A real devil!" He held her tightly, so tightly she could hardly catch her breath. She tried to pull away, but he was too strong. "You can try that self-defense now." He was forcing her face up to his and beginning to kiss her.

She longed to be strong-willed enough to pull away. But although he had called her a devil, it was he who was exerting the black magic, that old black magic, and she was sinking under the spell of it. The familiar feeling returned, the attraction he had held for her from their first meeting.

He kissed her, passionately, unrestrainedly, and she was beginning to respond totally, her confusion melting away. She felt enmeshed in a powerful, seductive web from which she was not sure she wanted to escape. Snatches of words he was murmuring now against her lips seemed to come from another person, in another voice entirely. Where was the cool scientist, always in control, keeping his distance?

She felt herself losing control but she knew she could not let it happen this way. She wanted love, not just physical attraction, and if Vic could ever feel for her the way she felt for him, she knew she would give herself to him without a second thought, her only desire to become one with him. But not like this, not when he wanted her out of anger.

With a final effort she managed to push him away, though her body ached for his touch and trembled with barely suppressed passion. "Please go now, Vic, please," she begged. Without a word he turned and walked out into the night.

CHAPTER EIGHT

THE NEXT MORNING she overslept and was barely able to arrive at the pier at the usual hour. There was no time to be embarrassed about what had almost happened the night before. She found that routine and Pepe's presence made everything seem almost normal. Almost. Vic's subdued, almost reflective mood at breakfast was definitely out of the ordinary, and she herself felt no desire to talk. Pepe's completely unmotivated repetition of "Man proposes, God disposes," came at them like a small bomb as they parted to get into their wet suits. Thank goodness they had been on their way to the deck when he had pronounced this dictum, as then there was no need to ask him what he meant by it.

The dive went unusually well. They picked up several remains of rusted-through metal objects held captive in coral deposits. The further they pushed through the sand-covered, hard-packed foundations of forgotten streets, the more they found and could collect for photographing and storing. She realized now that Vic could telescope his previous timetable, a thought he confirmed at lunch. Within another two weeks, he told her, they could close up shop. Then he could make the preparations with the Mexican government to have the area declared an archeological monument and staked off bounds until an expedition could be arranged.

Alex, still wrapped in her protective cloak of professionalism, refused to look ahead to define what the end of the project would mean to her. Last night had forced her to admit to herself that she loved Vic, and she was living intensely, hour by hour. Strangely, she found herself completely relaxed about the future as she carefully went about arranging on deck what she considered little crude pieces of rubble and photographing them from several angles. She knew they would later prove priceless, and at the moment this was her most important concern.

After two more submersions, there would be dinner and Ed's project to think about. She was relieved that the "invasion" would occupy her thoughts. Tonight she and Señora Davila must see to the ordering of the lamb, *con anticipación,* to be sure of the success of the barbecue. Then she must really make final that date for the yacht charter and contact the mariachi leader. Also there was the menu to plan for the day of the yacht affair. Then an entirely different boat had to be chartered for two or three game-fishing excursions. She welcomed the activity. It would take her mind off the fact that she felt hopelessly in love with a man who could not love her back. But the thought of his lips on hers, the memory of the strength of his desire, tormented her.

Was the Vic now on deck, helping with the shots she took, the same man who had almost made love to her just a few short hours before? She gave him a fleeting glance and captured the bronzed face totally concentrated on some object he was carefully turning in his hands. He was stripped to the waist, lean and sunburned across his broad shoulders and muscular biceps. Last night seemed so remote from this moment.

And yet, why did she feel somehow happy? What was the source of the new magic she felt inside? She felt on the verge of something undefined yet so large and mysterious that she knew she would be powerless to avoid it had she even wanted to. Is that what love is? she thought as she drove home to change for dinner.

Tired of faded, well-fitted jeans, Alex chose one of the attractive hand-blocked cotton print dresses she had been able to buy in one of the Sunday bazaars in the zócolo. She knew the cobalt-blue print became her and she deliberately arrived late to dinner, where she found the others waiting for her. The effect of her arrival was gratifying. Vic gave her a long, appraising look. Ed, rising and pulling out a chair for her, exclaimed over her dress, as did Jill. Alex sat down beside Ed and, after ordering, immediately went into a detailed review with him of her program for the visiting executives. He approved everything, from time to time consulting Jill and Don, and occasionally Marga, who managed to find just a little bit wrong with one or two items.

"You know best, Marga," Alex would say. "I'll change that."

Vic put in a word only now and then, giving the impression that he thought the entire project a bit frivolous.

"It's also a working vacation for these people," Don emphasized. "Some of them haven't had a real vacation in a couple of years. They're workaholics, most of them."

Vic looked into the distance with raised eyebrows.

"Now, the only other thing at the moment," Alex said to Ed, "is to check with Señora Davila about ordering the meat. We've got to do this in plenty of time so the butcher can do any necessary special ordering. That goes for the yacht party too, you know."

"Right." Ed beamed. "We'll get over to my place directly after dinner. Coming along, anyone? Vic—you and Marga?"

To Alex's surprise, Vic expressed a desire to join them—a decision which didn't seem to please Marga.

She was amused at Marga's expression as the brunette began to protest to Vic. Though she overheard him say something about Marga's having her own car, so she needn't go if she didn't want to, Alex gave no sign of having heard and continued to talk with Ed until it was time to leave.

"I'll follow you, Ed," she told him after saying good night to Don and Jill. She saw Vic rise, and gave a joint good night to him and Marga as though they were leaving together. But she knew they would probably both end up at Ed's house.

She was right. Even Jill and Don decided to come at the last minute. "Seems we can't do without each other," Jill said, laughing, as she sipped the brandy Mrs. Davila served them. She kicked off her shoes and sat down on the floor in front of the waterfall, where Don joined her.

Marga sat stiffly on one of the couches, next to Vic, who was watchful, somehow taking on the air of a chaperone, Alex was interested to see. She and Mrs. Davila settled down at one of the tables to confer, as Ed walked around, seeing that everyone was supplied with a full glass.

They discussed the weighty problem of mariachis versus a trio of guitars, or both taking turns. The pool must be serviced, the entire house turned out with the help of the gardener's wife, and more rose bushes had to be planted between the existing ones, because in January the blooms were sparser. Flowering bushes must be set in at once.

"So many details!" exclaimed Mrs. Davila happily. "But just wait and see how it all turns out—I promise you a success!"

Her enthusiasm transmitted itself to Alex, who was already inspired in quite another context. Later she looked up to see Don and Jill dancing—Jill in her stocking feet. Ed suggested that they must have covered everything by this time.

"Señora Davila will keep you all night if you let her," he told Alex. "Let's finish that dance we left hanging the other night at the Casa Madrid." He pulled her up, and they began to dance to the rhythm of one of Ed's collectors'-item discs.

Señora Davila gathered up her notes and prepared to leave after seeing that everyone was completely comfortable with drinks and the *bocadillos* she had provided.

"Hope Vic will give you at least one day free to help me with the affair," Ed said seriously. "He seems pretty uptight about your time."

"I've thought about that"—Alex nodded sagely—

"and I've decided that I'll run out of film just when your people arrive. Don't worry about it."

He breathed a sigh of relief.

"I'm having a good time, Ed," she said a little later, "but I'd really better leave after this dance. I think things will be okay now. We'll finish ordering tomorrow, and in case you see lots more people around the house, they'll be some of Mrs. Davila's relatives who are going to help."

"I thought it was going to be just a barbecue . . . or barbacoa, as it's supposed to be called."

"What? Just barbacoa? Not on your life! There'll be hand-made tortillas, guacamole, rice—Mexican rice—and there'll be a molé that takes two or three days to make."

"She's going to make up for lost time."

"I notice it's sort of customary down here. Look at Pepe's party the other night."

"And the food on the yacht you're renting?"

"That's going to be catered by the owners, but Mrs. Davila and I are going to choose the menu and oversee it just the same."

"So I don't have to worry?"

"Not about a thing. You're in good hands!"

"But suppose there's a 'norte' from Veracruz?"

"Ed—" she laughed, "I forbid you to worry about the weather!"

The day before the "invasion," Alex anticipated some trouble with Vic when she asked for time off. When told of the impending shortage of film, he replied tersely, "Yes, I thought this would happen about now. Especially timed for Ed's affair, I guess."

"I won't deny it." She smiled. "But you did say we were way ahead of schedule, and I notice your air tanks are getting low, too. Couldn't we coordinate restocking with Ed's affair? It means a lot to him."

"I know," he said, "and we can all use some relaxation."

She nodded, and could not help but be aware of his perfectly symmetrical body, naked except for brief swim shorts, evenly bronzed and exuding a magnetism that made her heart pound.

"I suppose I'd be a bad fellow if I didn't cooperate in this thing," he continued.

"How often does it happen?" she threw at him, sensing that ultimately he would give permission.

"Well, go ahead, for goodness' sake! Take the time off. Then I won't feel so guilty about what I said to Ed the other night."

"He thinks nothing of it," she replied, "and thanks for the time. You could use a couple of free days, too. We've been at it pretty steadily."

"I suppose so," he said, a surprisingly listless tone in his voice. "I feel great physically. It's just that sometimes things creep up on you, and before you know it, as simple as you try to keep things, there's a foul-up somewhere."

Alex tensed inwardly. It was possible he was worried about Marga. Maybe he cared about her more than he'd thought. Perhaps she was threatening to end their relationship because of Alex, and this was depressing him.

Alex reached for her weight belt and face plate

without comment, but her mood plunged into depression. He must be worried about Marga. What had almost passed between *them* recently was simply a forgotten incident in his life. He never even mentioned what had taken place in her casita. She had feared the worst, and now she knew it was true. That incendiary passion she felt for him was only a one-way attraction. For him it was simply temporary. She sighed and looked off into the never-ending horizon.

They came the next day—the "invasion" of ten pale, sun-dazzled executives. All of them admitted to suffering from jet lag and complete disorientation due to the sudden transition from gray skies, piles of dirty snow, cold winds and subzero temperatures in Massachusetts to blue skies, gentle winds, constant sunshine and friendly people in San Pablo.

"It's like passing from a black-and-white photograph to a color picture," the president said, bewildered. "Why, you even have roses in your patio. And don't tell me we can go on the beach! In January?"

Ed was expansive and glanced at Alex, silently congratulating her on accurately predicting how San Pablo would strike the group. "Why, of course we'll go to the beach, Fred," he replied as though he himself had invented the weather. "We do it every day. You're at sea level now, and in the tropic zone. We'll take advantage of that."

"But it was cold when we changed planes in Mexico City."

"Of course it was chilly. You were over a mile high

in the sky there. It makes a big difference," Ed explained.

They had just finished touring the plant on the afternoon of the barbecue. Everyone was scattered across the grounds, some by the pool, in bathing suits, others in shorts, looking with awe at the roses. Although all the men had traveled extensively, none of them could get over the change from brutally cold temperatures one day to paradise the next. Several were stretched out, trying to soak up as much sun as possible.

Alex and Marga circulated, supervising the waiters, who offered trays of large fresh coconuts, the tops of which were cut off to receive vodka, gin or tequila in the natural juice. Farther away, Chucho, surrounded by an astonished group of executives and five assistants, all relatives of Mrs. Davila, was carefully pulling back big banana leaves from an entire barbecued lamb, which had been slowly cooking over underground coals.

"You mean all that was under the ground?" Alex heard one visitor exclaim to Don.

"That's the real thing," he replied. "The space is carefully lined with banana leaves. The big pan is placed first for the consommé—the drippings. Then comes the lamb, and the leaves carefully folded over in a special design. Then lots of dirt on top. Underneath, of course, you've got the coals of fire."

"My gosh, but it smells delicious!"

"And that consommé is so rich, it's enough to make you whip your grandma!" another exclaimed as Chucho raised up the pan with the help of his assistants.

"He's got two more of these cooking," Alex told the group as she directed two helpers with a tray of gin-filled coconuts toward the group.

"And in a minute we're going to show you how to eat tacos," she promised, to the enthusiastic chorus of the group.

She was glad to see that Vic formed part of the crowd, having taken the day off, too. But she suspected that, aside from giving Ed his moral support, he was also there to keep an eye on Marga, who was constantly surrounded by a contingent of admirers.

Strolling musicians began strumming their guitars, and from the visitors Alex heard comments to the effect that few could remember as relaxed an afternoon as they were now spending. She saw Mrs. Davila, almost queenly in her black dress covered by a small white lace apron, directing various nieces, dressed in white aprons and caps. She was overseeing them most efficiently, never raising her voice, and seeming to be everywhere at once. Alex had also invited Pepe and his wife.

"Let us help you, Señorita," Pepe kept saying. "I can lend a hand here."

"Not on your life," Alex replied, laughing. "It's your turn to be a guest!"

She turned and saw Marga, completely in her element, surrounded by a small, admiring group of men who had obviously made her forget her hostessing and were plying her with what seemed to be questions about the cost of living in Mexico, particularly about retirement regulations. Well, Alex thought wryly, her own efforts were evidently successful. Who knows—

perhaps she'd induced some of the guests to fall permanently in love with Mexico.

Alex heard frequent laughter at some inside joke, and could see how changed the dark-haired woman was in the all-male circle as the center of attention. She blossomed to be twice as beautiful, Alex noticed, especially in that backless red cotton dress.

"Your purple print dress becomes you so much," Pepe's wife commented at this moment.

Alex gave a start, wondering if the other woman had read her mind. "Thanks, Señora," she replied. "You don't know how great you made me feel!"

After the buffet, which seemed a revelation to the guests, the mariachis filed in and drowned out conversation. Folk dancers suddenly appeared as if from nowhere and began a *raspa* to the music of Veracruz, as later the white-clad Veracruz musicians appeared with their special stringed instruments.

"I never expected anything like this," the company president told Ed. "Why, this is a banquet and a spectacle all in one!"

"It's really nothing." Ed smiled, with a wink at Alex, nearby. "Only what you folks deserve. We have it every day—you people up there in Massachusetts are the ones suffering. Now for a few days you can see how the other half lives."

"I don't see how you can get so much done with all this to enjoy."

"This is only the beginning," Alex answered. "Tomorrow we go sailing. And if anyone wants to go to the bottom, I'll be the guide."

"I'll stay with the ship." The president laughed.

"And I'll keep you company," Ed added. "This young lady is a pro diver, as I told you, John, but what I didn't tell you is that she arranged all this for us. I didn't really have a thing to do with the social goings-on."

"You're a genius!" John told Alex. "Any time you tire of diving, let me know—always a job up in Pittsfield for you."

As they all laughed, Alex noted that Marga, in one of her rare moments alone, had joined the group behind her. When Alex turned, she surprised a flash of raw jealousy on Marga's face, which swiftly changed as one of the men took her arm to draw her in.

Alex left to see to the other guests and later to change for a swim in the pool. She knew the day had gone well, beyond Ed's fondest hopes, and she knew that such a good start presaged success for the other two days of the "invasion."

CHAPTER NINE

THE YACHT TRIP that afternoon was enhanced by a calm sea and very clear, cobalt-blue skies. The dining room on board featured a complete buffet, which was periodically replenished. Two alternating groups provided continuous music, and as the yacht followed the coastline up past Tierra Quemada the visitors gasped at the beauty and serenity of the landscape.

Nobody wanted to go scuba diving, so Alex stayed on the yacht and helped Jill and Marga supervise the activities. Although it was a busy time for the three of them, Alex was aware that Marga took the role of leader whenever their paths crossed, usually directing her to do something insignificant, and occasionally trying to do the same to Jill. At the same time she managed to be all things to each one of the guests and was frequently surrounded by a crowd of admirers, who seemed to hang on her words.

"She's a knockout!" Alex heard one of them comment. "Brains and beauty together! What a combo!"

"Marga's the belle of the ball," Jill whispered to Alex. "She's practically holding court."

Alex laughed. "I wonder if I should've been born brunette—tall and striking instead of medium and blond!"

"Are you kidding?" Jill almost yelped. "With *your* looks—and when everybody keeps tinting their hair blond like ours? Of course, these days I have to beef mine up a little. Time marches on, you know."

At the end of the third day, which had included big-game fishing for some of the committee, a tired but happy and slightly sunburned group headed for the airport in several cars, more than contented with the new plant and with their vacation. Alex was pleased that several had seriously decided to look into the retirement policies of the country, more than ever wondering why they had to stay in a cold climate much of the winter.

After their departure, Ed gathered his circle in his living room and pressed glasses of champagne into their hands.

"What is there to say?" he demanded, raising his glass in a toast. "To the best group of people in the world—who made it a howling success!"

They drank. Ed continued, "To you first, Alex, who planned the social part!"

Alex saw the quick, furious glance Marga directed at her, but ignored it as they all drank again.

"To you, my dear Jill and Don, my right hand, as I always say! And Vic—you're the best, to stop all your plans and rally round the cause, even risking your lovely Marga among all those wolves!"

They began to post-mortem the three days' activities, Ed and Don referring to events at the plant, the others concentrating on the social activities and the visitors' unexpected enthusiasm.

"They were stunned," Don reminisced. "Frankly, I had forgotten how pale we all were up in the Northeast. The winter sunshine down here really got to them."

Marga snuggled next to Vic on a divan, drawing her legs under her. "And a couple of them tried to get to me," she informed them. "I can have any position at the main plant any time I want to." She looked at Ed.

"Don't let me stand in your way, Marga," he replied, "but just remember who gave a pretty woman credit for brains and never mixed business with fooling around. Remember who gave you your start!"

"Oh, can't you take a joke anymore?" Marga laughed.

"Yeah, but that was pretty close to home," Ed retorted.

Alex noticed that Marga's hand was patting Vic's as she murmured something the others could not hear—probably assuring him that nothing could ever come between them, she guessed.

"Oh, you two people," Jill chided Ed. "Why spoil a wonderful success?"

"That's what I say," seconded Don. "Marga, you were wonderful. Enjoy it, then forget it!"

Mrs. Davila came in to announce that a small supper would shortly be served on the patio.

"How does she do it?" Jill wondered aloud as they all made the move to the softly lit area, where the white wrought-iron round table was loaded with what seemed to be a smorgasbord with Mexican overtones.

"She's been wasted all this time! I'm going to start

entertaining more!" Ed declared.

Vic and Marga, hand in hand, followed, with Alex and Ed trailing them. For Alex, the supposedly triumphant celebration was losing its shine. What could have been the icing on the cake was now dissolving into nothing for her as she watched the frequent little possessive gestures between Vic and Marga.

It was late when she finally drove home to the casita. She anticipated a short session of reading in bed, propped up on pillows, lulled by the champagne and the good supper into forgetting her depression, and then dropping off to sleep. But shortly after turning off her reading lamp, she heard the beginning of the soft, lazy but powerful approach of a motor which she could never fail to recognize. But no, it couldn't be—how was it possible? Yet as the sound slowly increased in volume, purring a little louder now, she sat up abruptly, almost bewildered. It couldn't be the Masarati—*the* Masarati! It was against all the laws of probability. She must be mistaken.

Yet deep inside her she knew there was no denying the unique sound of that specially built motor. She and Conrad had ordered it to his specifications, in Rome, on their honeymoon. But Conrad here in San Pablo? No way! She sprang from bed and looked out of the window at the approaching shadow. There it came with that slow, arrogant, low growl of a perfectly adjusted machine, pampered as only Conrad would pamper it. Now it came into view, gliding almost past her house, but then backing up, and she knew now that it would unfailingly stop in front. It did. The lights were turned off, the door slammed, and there was Conrad, leaning against the car door, gazing at the house.

She could easily make out his silhouette in the moonlight, and then heard the crunch of gravel as he came slowly walking up her pathway. Hurriedly she threw on her robe, caught completely off balance. He was the last person in the world she would ever have expected in San Pablo, and she couldn't remember the last time she had thought of him. He seemed to have materialized from some distant, unpleasant dream—very distant. An eternity seemed to pass before the knock came. She turned on the lights and opened the door.

"Hi, kid," he greeted her, as though they had parted only an hour ago.

She stared at him a moment before answering. "Quite a surprise visit, wouldn't you say?"

He entered the room and looked around, summing up the small area before sitting at the table. He's the same, Alex thought as she studied him. The assured, arrogant manner that being rich from childhood so often brought, blond hair still cut Italian style, long in the back, the too-handsome features not so cleancut now, with only a hint of weakness at the mouth. He wore Paris-tailored jeans cut to his figure, and a shirt deeply opened to display the gold chains against an evenly tan chest.

"What the hell are you doing in this dump?" he began, crossing his legs as he lit a cigarette with his gold lighter.

She sat down opposite him and smiled indulgently. "Gosh, Con, you sure know how to make a knockout entrance. And so romantic."

He ignored her remark. "Or is this just some of your reverse snobbism?" he continued, still looking around. "God knows you're not strapped for money. But this is going too far, Alex."

"Look, Con, I'm on a job. I work, remember?" She felt a sudden anger. To be invaded after midnight by the person who had upset her whole life, and then to be criticized for her temporary surroundings was just too much. "And it was a job that gave me the change I needed after your recent performance."

He decided not to pursue that issue. After a short pause he said, "Don't tell me there's no scotch on hand. I've had a hell of a drive over these damn gravel roads, looking for you."

"No. There's no scotch. But there's some brandy I keep for emergencies, if you want it."

"Well give me *something*, for God's sake," he muttered.

She poured him the brandy and sat down again, waiting for his explanation. He drank it in two swallows and pushed the glass away.

"Guess you're wondering why I showed up." He smiled, and it was the old captivating smile.

"Naturally," she replied briefly, firmly resolving that his old charm would move her no longer.

"Can't you take a guess?" He pushed his glass forward for more brandy, which she poured.

"After midnight, with a full day of diving ahead tomorrow, I'm not exactly set up to play guessing games. But it couldn't be anything related to the divorce—that was squared away before I left. You're completely free. As I remember, it was Wendy Wells you were last squiring around—the latest bombshell of Apex studios."

"Oh, for the love of Pete, Alex—that was only a hot minute!" He gave his little-boy grin.

She began to laugh, remembering how often that smile had formerly gotten around her. "Was it too hot not to cool down?" she finally asked.

"Now you've got it, kid," he replied, sipping his brandy.

"Well, were there some loose ends to tie up between us? Anything you want me to sign?"

"Not really, Alex. I just wanted you to know I've been thinking a lot since you left—and why the hell did you leave so soon? You didn't even say goodbye."

"Oh, like in the movies, when they play those memory songs and we're supposed to fade out with tears—was that what you wanted?"

He lowered his eyes, aware of her cynicism. "You know damn well I don't mean that. What I mean is you didn't give me a chance!"

"I didn't give you a chance! Conrad, how much more of a chance did you want? You had every chance, and you took them all. I lost count of the women you fooled around with while we were married." Suddenly she remembered Pepe's theory. "What you really needed was more flings. Now you've got the freedom to do what you want."

He gave his crooked grin, which she also remembered. Tilting his chair back and looking at the ceiling, he said, "Guess what! Maybe I don't want all that freedom anymore."

Alex stared at him in surprise.

"You know what, Con?" she began slowly. "Some people would rather enjoy things when they know they're wrong. They don't get a kick out of them when they're the right thing to do. I wonder if that's your problem."

"What the hell do you mean, Alex?" he flared. "I drive down here to this Godforsaken town, bad roads ruining my tires and my shocks, asking all over again for you to try to make everything all right, and here you are calling me names!"

He was still the same. He had always had the knack of putting her in the wrong and pretending to be deeply hurt.

"Trying to make everything all right again?" she asked.

"Why else would I come? There wasn't that much wrong with us in the first place. It was you who got up in arms about a couple of things that didn't amount to a hill of beans. *You* made a mountain out of a molehill! We could've made it. You didn't want it to work!" He flung the words at her.

"I guess it was all my fault?"

He had the grace to hedge. "Well, why don't we let bygones be bygones, Alex? Let's don't rehash all that. To be frank, I came here to see if we couldn't patch things up."

"I never liked patchwork, Con," she told him..

"Don't be so smart, Alex," he replied, coming around and standing over her. "You know what I mean. We've known each other a long time, since we were kids—we belong together. Can't you overlook a few little slips? They didn't mean anything."

"But they hurt a lot just the same," she said. "I just didn't know how marriage to you actually would be."

"But my mother forgave my father lots worse than that!"

"That was your mother," she replied quietly. "If that was how she handled all that infidelity, it must have been right for her."

"But not for you?"

"No."

During the stalemate he took his seat again and, finishing his brandy, he lit a fresh cigarette.

"What kind of a dive are you on?" he asked casually.

"I'm working with an archeologist," she replied.

"An archeologist!" he commented, making no secret of his disdain. "Down this way you could bring up some Spanish galleons. Plenty sunk in these waters."

"I know."

He suddenly came around to her again and pulled her up. "Alex, what happened to us? Don't we still love each other?" He drew her to him. As he kissed her, she remembered the old days, when he could make her believe he would be hers alone. Purposely she accepted his kiss, but she felt nothing. It was all dead between them—gone. She was sure now that his old charm could no longer work its magic on her.

"Remember those nights on the beach when—"

"I've tried to forget them, Con," she interrupted.

"Why? Why?" he repeated, seeming to be genuinely hurt as he held her away from him.

"Because it was better that way," she told him, allowing him to kiss her again before she gently pulled away. "And we're divorced, remember?"

"You can never forget me," he whispered in her ear. "All those things we shared..."

"Before we were married," she reminded him. "Afterwards you shared them with others."

"Oh, Alex, you're so stubborn! You're a damn puritan!" He pushed her away and sat down again.

"Con," she said, still standing, "I'm sorry, but I'm not the naïve girl I was when we married. How many times did you tell me I was a spoilsport, that I made you a drudge in our diving business?...Now you can have all the fun you want, but please don't put me in the same role again—I know what I want in a man, and what I need."

"I told you I've changed...."

"Nobody could change that much. Of course I have memories, some good and some bad, but the bad ones were pretty awful. Let's just be friends, okay?"

He stood and began pacing the room. "You'll be sorry, Alex Wood! You'll want to come back, and it just may be too late!"

She suppressed a smile. "That's a risk I'll have to take."

"Then, I take it the answer is no?" he asked unbelievingly.

"That's right—at the moment, anyway," she qualified, to preserve some of his pride.

"At the moment?" He caught at the hope right away.

"Right."

"Well, Alex, I've done everything I could. You're just about impossible. But if you want me back, you'd better make up your mind pretty soon. Tomorrow I'm driving on to Merida to do some spear fishing, and then back to California."

"I see."

"Any hotels in this Godforsaken spot? I can't risk the Masarati in pitch dark on these roads." He sat down and poured himself more brandy.

"Not that I know of. You'll have to go into Tierra Quemada for a room." She had remained standing, hoping to encourage his departure, but now she was forced to sit down and wait for him to finish his drink.

"You mean that flea-bitten building I passed on the main square of the last town? The sign on it said hotel, but all I could see was a two-story adobe dump."

"There might be a couple of motels nearby," she suggested.

He looked at his watch. "It's going on two in the morning now. If you think I'm going to forage around this time of night in God knows what kind of situation there'd be in a foreign country—maybe risking my life—you're crazy!"

"What would you suggest?" she asked, her heart sinking.

"If you had any kind of feeling at all, Alex, you'd let me stay. That is—unless you have other plans for tonight—visitors, maybe? Maybe—"

"That's enough of that, Con! Get off that track. You can see I don't have much space here—"

"I see a nice little bed over in that alcove—it's a single, but—"

"But what?" Alex challenged, leveling her gaze at him.

"Well—anyway, I've got my sleeping bag in the car," he grumbled. "You sure know how to welcome a guy, Alex."

She was torn between anger and amusement. "Oh, was I supposed to be waiting all this time, hoping you'd return, keeping the light in the window—"

She stopped as he slammed angrily out of the door to get his overnight necessities. In a few moments he returned and, after throwing her a hurt glance, silently began preparing a pallet—on the floor. He made a show of taking his overnight bag into the small bathroom, emerging shortly, modestly wrapped in an obviously expensive lightweight silk robe. Meanwhile Alex had placed one of her extra pillows for him and was preparing to get into her own bed.

"I hope I'm not inconveniencing you," he said almost haughtily, approaching her sleeping alcove.

"Since it's more or less an emergency for one night, what can I do about it?" she answered, reluctant to get into bed with him standing near.

He sat down on her bed and looked earnestly at her as she stood beside the small night table. "Alex," he pleaded, "don't wait too long to decide about coming back. I know we might have had problems, but just think—we've known each other for such a long time. I always knew we'd marry. We belong together."

"Yes, you said that before." She gave up hope for a good night's sleep. "But it's late now, so let's shelve it. I've got to be on the job early."

He stood up and in one sweep took her in his arms. "Alex, give me another chance!" He began kissing her, while she remained impassive, unmoved by the remembered techniques. He was still sure of himself, sure she would capitulate, as she had so often done before, she realized.

But as she had pointed out to him earlier, she was different now. And the contrast between the deep, magnetic attraction of Vic, and Con's ineffectual, almost immature aura underscored for her just how much she'd changed. She disentangled herself silently, and pointedly remained standing until he gave a helpless shrug and went to his sleeping bag. She heard him pound the pillow and wrap himself in his sleeping bag, giving a sigh of self-pity. Then she at last got into bed, to sleep restlessly for the few shorts hours left to her.

CHAPTER TEN

HAVING GOTTEN CONRAD'S promise to leave early that morning, she managed to get to the *Vera* at the usual time. As she parked her car behind the jeep, near the pier, she noticed that Vic was already on board. Once she was on deck, the welcome fragrance of cooking bacon came to her. Pepe, aware of her presence, called out that it was breakfast-time, and she waited until Vic silently entered the room.

He stood a moment looking speculatively at her before coldly returning her greeting. For the first time it occurred to her that perhaps he had seen the car in front of her house and had thought she was entertaining a casual friend—that she was promiscuous. But what business was it of his even if that were the case?

Yet she felt a strong urge to explain to him what had happened. As they ate and listened to Pepe's comments about the recent doings for the visitors, Alex pondered how best to introduce the subject. Finally she took advantage of one of Pepe's absences from the table to mention, somewhat self-consciously, Conrad's visit.

"An unexpected visitor came along last night," she told Vic. "My ex-husband, Conrad."

Vic did not raise his eyes from his plate as he answered, "Yes, I saw the car there—and the California license plates."

She was surprised to realize that he had been near enough to read the plates on the car.

"Naturally, hearing the car and seeing it stop at your door made me go out to check," he said as he finished his breakfast and rose to leave. "After all, I didn't realize at first who it was—whether you needed help. Keeping you safe is my problem, after all." His tone was curt as he left to change into his wet suit, without giving her a chance to answer.

So he had come to check, she pondered. He had guessed that it was Conrad from the license plates—but how much had he seen? And then, of course, the car was in front of the house all night. In fact, it was there when they had both left in the morning for the boat, she remembered with a slight shudder. What did it matter what he thought, in any case? she wondered. Marga and he seemed to be quite close now. Was he such a prig as to judge her even if he did think she and her ex-husband had slept together? And in these days of permissiveness?

She almost cried out aloud—unfair, unfair—and was surprised to find herself fighting back tears of frustration. Why did this man have the knack of making her helplessly angry? How could she explain to him that she hadn't slept with Conrad, that he had stayed on the floor, in his sleeping bag, that he was now less than nothing to her. Could she tell him that he, Victor Clarke, was the man she loved, and had loved for some time, that he was the only man whose kisses could make her vibrate with passion?

She looked up to see Pepe smiling at her. She had not noticed him enter, and suspected he had been looking at her for some time.

"I better hurry to get into my wet suit," she mumbled, scrambling up.

"Man proposes, God disposes," she heard Pepe murmur as she left. For some reason the saying upset her more than ever and made her wonder if he wasn't aware of some of the recent dilemmas.

She passed Vic on her way down the deck, but he gave no sign of having seen her, as he continued carefully rubbing some rusty figurine, his head remaining bent when she passed by. In spite of her bold resolves, just passing him reminded her of how much she cared for him. Had he turned to reach out for her, how gladly would she have gone into those bronzed arms, leaned against his hard muscular chest and accepted his kisses—even now, she would have. Hesitating but a moment beside him, she continued on to prepare for the dive as he turned to go in the opposite direction.

Later she was glad when they both, suited and masked, slipped over backward into the waiting blue-green water. At least the dive would fill her mind, making her forget both Vic, and Con's untimely visit. And the natural lack of vocal communication underwater would make her forget, even if just temporarily, Vic's new coldness toward her. They would be just two rubber-suited people—he the scientist, she the diver and photographer, exploring the forgotten city where tragedy had long ago struck—tragedy far more cataclysmic than theirs would ever be.

Yet for her some of the joy of the dive seemed

diminished. The same hand signals, the same slow pushing ahead with stops to take the pictures Vic indicated, the same schools of curious fish nudging her at intervals, the same careful avoidance of the occasional stingray, half buried in the sand . . . none of it excited her any longer. Vic found two items which could later be examined and might prove of value. Under ordinary circumstances the discovery would have cheered her, but now she felt depressed, jaded.

Lunchtime brought no change. Vic spoke only when necessary, addressing himself mainly to Pepe, who, she was glad to see, helped bridge the strained relations with his apt comments and occasional stories.

On deck after lunch Vic occupied himself with examining his finds of the morning. When she looked over his shoulder to see them, he turned and with a grunted "Take them," gave them to her, walking away to his deck chair, which he had pulled away from hers. She looked down at the two pieces which she could not have differentiated in the normal way from two clumps of hardened mud, and carefully set them in a sheltered spot to silently photograph. A short nap made her feel better physically, and she awoke to find that Vic was already in his wet suit, waiting for her at the rail. She started up to change for the afternoon dive.

"I imagine you could sleep longer," he said as she passed him, "having had a rather busy night!"

She flushed deeply and before thinking, retorted, "Perhaps we both did!"

Yet as she changed into her suit, she regretted her words, which seemed to verify what he already thought about her. Then she became angry with herself for caring. She was beginning to hate him—and to hate herself.

The afternoon dive went well, as they moved farther and farther into the maze of the city. Determined that he would not be able to accuse her of inefficiency, Alex was more than ever on the alert, springing into action when he gave the signal, asking only that he occasionally hold the strobes for her.

She would show him how clever she was—how cool and impersonal she could be if that was the way he wanted it. She would continue to be helpful to show him how little she cared whether he was or was not civil to her.

Back at the pier, she was first off the boat, in order to get home for her shower, thankful for the independence her own car gave her. She dreaded going to dinner with the group, but dreaded more finding Conrad still around. As she rounded the ocean-front road, she was relieved to see no sign of the car. Thank God. He was one complication she didn't need. She had created enough for herself already. If only she could invent some excuse for not eating at the same table with Vic and Marga.

She found she need not have worried, however. As she left the house, ready for dinner, she saw Ed's car coming toward her. She waited for him to stop, not sure whether he was going farther up, to Vic's house, or not.

"I was trying to catch you before you left," he told her, leaning out. "Hop in—we're not gathering tonight. Vic and Marga are eating in Tierra Quemada, and Don and Jill are making a New England dinner at home. We're invited, of course—but I owe you, Alex, and I want to invite you to a real gourmet treat for a change."

Alex hesitated, glad her problem was solved yet unhappy about Vic and Marga's tête-à-tête. "I need something special, Ed." She smiled, stepping into his car. "I'm in a bit of a blue funk after having the people from your plant down here."

"Me, too." He laughed, driving off. "It was so terrific that the bottom seemed to fall out when they left. We can go into Tierra Quemada, too, but there's a special place I want you to try. Not with Vic and Marga—I need to get a rest from my staff sometimes."

Relieved, Alex wondered just how much Ed had been able to guess about her feelings for Vic. But his next remark indicated that perhaps her feelings weren't as obvious as she feared.

"Not that Marga isn't in fine fettle today," Ed added, "what with dining and maybe dancing tonight with Vic—away from us. But just the same, we all need an occasional rest from one another."

Alex felt further depressed with this additional information. But hadn't she decided not to care? "I suppose it's hard not to be together, when you're practically the only people in town who speak English," she managed to answer, quelling her feelings.

"That's just it. Who wants to eat alone—or eat with somebody Mexican and have to worry about subjunctives in Spanish all evening after doing it all day? That's why we're together so much—necessity."

Again the beautiful scenery struck her in a bittersweet fashion. How she would have enjoyed it with someone she loved—someone who cared for her, too—who reciprocated her affection and valued her. Ed was a lifesaver, but she found herself answering him with one part of her mind while thinking of Vic and Marga being together with the other part. Just the same, as Ed pulled up in front of a small white building almost hidden by flowering trees, she was able to snap out of her doldrums and appreciate what he was saying.

"It's French," he announced. "*Really* French. The owner is the chef and came from Provence. You'll love it! I promise."

Enjoy it she did, to her surprise, forgetting everything for the moment and responding to the special attention the chef and his wife gave the two of them.

"You took the trouble to call and make the reservation," the tall white-capped owner said to Ed, "and that makes all the difference. I have everything on hand—and by plane came my precious *foie gras* from Strasbourg—not pâté, mind you, but the actual *foie!*" He spoke in French-accented Spanish.

"We're in luck!" Ed beamed at Alex.

"I can't imagine it—this terrific place being in Tierra Quemada," she answered.

"Just one thing!" the chef warned. "Do me the favor to let me choose your wines. None of this tequila to paralyze the palate, mind you!"

Ed and Alex exchanged glances—no margaritas this evening.

"We are in your hands, François," Ed told him. "Whatever you say."

The evening really made Alex forget her problems, to her delight. As course after course was almost lovingly served by Madame herself, they saw that François had extended himself for them. Other patrons in the small place looked at them curiously, realizing who were tonight's favored ones.

Alex was in bed early, appreciating Ed more than ever. They had eaten leisurely, savored the correct wines chosen for them with every course, and accepted the aged cognac afterwards with the matchless dessert, also chosen for them by the omnipotent François.

Now, drifting off to a well-deserved sleep, Alex wondered vaguely why so many pleasant experiences had to have a kind of inborn flaw. The same evening with the wonderful mythical person who returned her love would have been more than memorable. She ignored the fact that her invented person always took on the physical characteristics of Vic. It was strange, since she had decided that she hated him. He had failed to speak a civil word to her that whole working day, and the put-down about her being busy the night before was inexcusable.

A motor sounded in the distance, and her heart accelerated. It was the jeep. So he was home early from his dinner-dancing date with Marga. She heard the vehicle passing her house and stopping at his. A door slammed, and all was silent. She turned toward the wall and finally found sleep.

The next two days were strained for Alex, who at first found it difficult walking the tightrope between civility and coolness with Vic. His manner had become even more reserved with her, and hardened her resolve not to explain anything about Conrad's visit.

Using the excuse of making some long-distance

calls to her family in California, she had managed to avoid the usual gathering for dinner. As there was only one telephone in San Pablo where these calls could be made, it was easy to convince everyone. She actually did make her calls, and later ate alone at another restaurant.

It was therefore surprising to her when, on the third day after Conrad's visit, on arriving at the pier, she found Vic waiting for her beside his jeep. She parked while he moved toward her, and again she marveled at the sense of quiet strength of which his every action spoke.

"The notice came about that film you ordered," he said curtly, without a greeting. "It's passed customs in Mexico City and has to be picked up at the post office in Tierra Quemada—that is, unless you want to wait a week more for it to arrive in San Pablo."

"Heaven forbid," she replied, getting back into her car. "If it's okay with you, I'll pick it up now."

"I'm going in for the other air tanks I ordered, and to pick up some clothes. If you want to come along with me in the jeep—"

"But couldn't you pick up my film at the same time?"

"Don't you know by now that since it's in your name you have to come in person and show your passport? And there'll be a tax on it, too, by the way." His tone was gruff as he turned away toward the jeep.

She sat stunned for a moment, wondering what to do. It would be so nice to go ahead without him—to pay him back for that surly speech. Yet she heard him start the motor, and without giving herself time to think further, she quickly left her car and went to get in beside him.

"We can have breakfast there," he said as he maneuvered the car expertly past the pedestrians now beginning to come along to the pier. "But I like to get an early start when there's business like this to take care of."

She remained silent, having decided that he deserved only the briefest of replies.

"Pepe's still going over the motor," he added, "so we're not losing any time."

Still she did not comment, noticing that he had taken the scenic road to Tierra Quemada—the very road she had so often wanted to travel with him. And now here they were, and as usual there was a flaw in what should have been a pleasure—the way things now were between them. She watched the early-morning sun reflect on the moving ocean and realized it was the first time she had taken this route in the daytime. It showed another kind of beauty now—delicate, with rose and gold tones still showing in the sky after the recent sunrise.

Lazy gulls circled around the white sailboats, and far in the distance, clouds gilded by the sun drifted out to sea. The air was brisk, still fresh, as yet free of the sun's touch. The road was filled with fragrant blooming cactus on the mountainside. She found it almost painful not to comment—to have to hold in her deeply felt response to the scene. It would be a relief to share it with someone—but how could she volunteer anything to the man sitting beside her?

She stole a glance at him and suddenly felt a familiar

magic overcome her. What was it—the strong profile, the characteristic wave of the dark hair, tending to fall over one eye at times, the open, short-sleeved shirt that revealed the hard biceps, the strong neck and chest...

"I hope this won't inconvenience you, or anything," he suddenly said, almost making her jump.

"Inconvenience me? I don't know what you mean by that. I need the film as soon as possible—for your work."

He glanced at her significantly. "I mean with your husband."

"My husband? My *ex*-husband?" she repeated, surprised.

"Don't give me that!" he shot back at her. "I mean I hope this ride together won't get you in trouble with your ex-husband...or the man you were kissing the other night by the window...the man with the Masarati parked in front of your door. Plain enough now?"

She was taken aback for a moment. So he had seen them—Con's forced kisses, which she had never returned, the embrace from which she had disengaged herself as soon as possible.

"Frankly," she began, at last able to yield to the urge to explain, "he *did* kiss me, but—"

"I know he did," Vic interrupted, "because when I went down to check the car to see if you were all right, there were your silhouettes, plain as day against the window. You two would do well in Hollywood. I figured you didn't need any help at all."

The surging words tumbled against themselves as she replied angrily, "Yes, he did kiss me! After all, he *was* my husband. But I fail to see what *you* have to do with it. Do I go around snooping when you take Marga wining, dining and dancing? Do I comment when she gives that sickening 'You're the boss, darling?'" Here she gave an imitation of Marga's tone. "Do I go peeping in the windows of *your* house—or *her* house!" She stopped, angry and breathless.

"Hey, wait a minute there, Alex." He slowed the car and stared at her. "I didn't go snooping, as you call it. Here we are in another country, with other customs. You're living alone, down the road from me. A car drives up. It was my duty to check it out. Then, when I went up to knock on your door, I couldn't help but see you against the window. With that kind of car and that California plate, I guessed it was either your husband—I mean ex-husband—or a very good friend, so I went away."

She turned her head to cool her face, to hide the strong emotion she did not wish him to see.

"I figured he'd come to get you back again, when I saw how well you were getting along," he added.

"He did come for that," she said, to show him that she, too, was wanted in marriage—not just for a casual affair.

"Ah—I thought that." He nodded, picking up speed again. "And of course that explains why the car stayed there all night."

Her sense of fairness, combined with her pride, forbade her to explain. Let him think what he would.

"And how did you enjoy *your* outing last night?" she asked. "How would you like it if I tried to keep tabs on you like that?"

"Oh, I wouldn't mind at all," he said maddeningly. "We had a wonderful time. Had dinner at the Casa

Madrid again. They've changed their show, you know. You and Ed should go there next time—or you and your husband—whichever."

She felt the same mixture of anger and frustration and did not trust herself to speak as she looked blindly out at the exquisite scenery. So he knew about her dinner with Ed—not that it was any secret. It was just so infuriating that under the cover of protecting her he was subtly criticizing her. It was probably his New England upbringing—that puritanism. Ed was married, and she supposed Vic thought she shouldn't have gone out alone with him. And also she was not now married to Con, and Vic thought she had been intimate with him without benefit of clergy. But then, it was okay for him to practically seduce her—or was it that? What about her part in their embraces, before she'd had the strength to stop them? Downing this uncomfortable thought, she continued, yes, it was all right if *he* gave in to his own caprices, but *she* should walk the straight and narrow! The old double standard again.

"Well, no need to be so glum," Vic said. "We're almost there. After the post office, I'll treat you to breakfast—it's really the least I can do. Thanks to you, I'll soon be able to announce the find to the scientific community. And I especially feel like a fool after treating you so badly when you first arrived."

He reached out and squeezed her hand. "Truce?"

Oh, why not, she thought. This little outing would probably be one of their last times together, so she might as well enjoy it.

She smiled at him. "Truce," she agreed.

CHAPTER ELEVEN

THEIR FIRST STOP was the post office. Vic waited for her, afterwards leading her to some pleasant outdoor tables, where they were served a Mexican breakfast of fruit, coffee and eggs *ranchero*. They talked pleasantly about the beauty of the town in the early morning, and Alex was filled with a sense of poignancy. They were capable of getting along so well. Why did it have to end so soon?

"Do you want to come with me for the tanks?" he asked as they finished.

She considered. She could window-shop, looking at more embroidered blouses and dresses, but she found herself walking along beside him toward the supply place where they usually stocked up. The morning was so pleasant, the little square lined with trees so inviting, the bougainvillaea vines so brilliant against the white adobe shops and houses, that Alex felt totally relaxed and almost started to hum.

"I've got to pick out some more shirts and jeans," he said, heading for a nearby store. "Do you mind? Or would you rather rest on a bench in the park over there?"

"Rest! No, I need the exercise," she protested, not anxious to be left alone, away from him.

"Maybe you can help me," he said as they entered

the place. "Nowadays there's a choice down here."

The heady smell of denim was pleasant as she was led into the small shop piled high on all sides with heavy, practical workingmen's clothes. There was so much merchandise that it was hard to see the attendant. Finally a smiling teen-age boy appeared, seeming to recognize Vic.

Alex watched as the boy pulled out several styles of jeans and shirts in Vic's size, efficiently selling the whole time, explaining the advantages of buying more than one pair of pants, and how hard it was to get in a shipment of the heavy ones. The boy explained that his mother had just delivered a little brother, and his father and the other children were at the hospital, visiting her, so he was in charge. She watched Vic's manner with him, never condescending, always man to man. He haggled only a little on the price.

"I'm no match for you, Beto," Vic ended up as he accepted a compromise. "You'll be rich, and very soon, at this rate!"

Beto protested that prices had gone up wholesale and that he really was giving Vic the lowest possible terms because he was a regular customer.

"Yes, and that's what you tell all the customers!" Vic laughed, and Beto laughed with him. Alex found herself smiling and filled with a sense of total contentment at being able to share such a warm moment with Vic.

As they went out into the bright sunshine, he hesitated, looking to the right of the store. "There used to be a 'market on wheels' on that street down there."

He pointed. "If you want to see it, come along. It's only on Tuesdays."

"Market on wheels?" she repeated, following him.

"Yes, that's right. A market that is set up one day a week, with the small merchants selling everything from produce to clothes, meat, plants and silver."

They found it, and Alex saw that it dazzled the eye. Gaudy cheap dresses and aprons were hanging side by side with some of the most exquisite embroidered ponchos; next to that stand was a butcher cutting up hunks of beef, hawking his wares at the same time; then came a stand of cheap jewelry with flashing red and green stones side by side with the handmade heavy silver pieces beautifully engraved and worked; then the copper work, vases from every province, including Oaxaca and Tonalá; and now a jungle of palm plants and leafy philodendrons boasting the largest leaves she had ever seen. Amid the people, becoming more numerous every moment, Alex felt Vic take her hand. He pulled her from the path of some housewives trundling their shopping carts, but once she was safe, he did not let go of her.

"See anything you want here?" he asked as they moved slowly along, both of them totally relaxed, luxuriating in their nearness.

"A million things!" she answered. "I want some of those blouses over there—the embroidered ones, and those dresses back there at the first stand we passed."

"Well, why didn't you say so! We'll go back—"

"It's just that I didn't bring any money with me. I didn't know we were coming here today. It was just lucky I had my passport in my tote bag."

"That's no problem," he assured her. "I have some money."

"Just as an advance on my next week's salary," she insisted.

He grinned at her. "Okay."

He handed her a roll of what turned out to be ten hundred-peso bills, and they headed back to bargain for the dresses she wanted. Vic instructed her not to show too much enthusiasm, as that would increase the price. She obeyed as he played the part of the totally disinterested, not-too-approving husband. She glowed with pleasure, caught up in the magic of their charade. The same technique was used on the blouses, at which point Alex found her money running out.

"I was hoping I'd have enough for one of those big brass pots," she mentioned as they passed them slowly. "I'd like to give Jill and Don at least one for their living room. They've decorated it with a brass motif."

"Now's the time," Vic advised. "You don't get over here very often in the daytime, and the market takes place only on Tuesdays."

"But I'm fresh out of money and don't want to use all yours—you might want to buy something, too."

"The jeans and shirts were my only luxury," he said, reaching into his pocket again. "Here, take this other thousand pesos and get what you want—only be sure to bargain well. I could have knocked fifteen more pesos off that last blouse you bought."

"Then *you* bargain for the brass things," she suggested.

"Sure; watch me."

She observed, fascinated, as Vic stopped at the orange-juice stand next to the brass merchant and casually looked around as he bought two cups, handing her one. The seller of the pots caught Vic's eye and began his pitch. As the pots were lined up on the pavement, Vic gently nudged one with his toe and in Spanish asked Alex if she wanted one. Alex, by now wiser, answered, "Not particularly."

"This is expected of us," Vic said in English. "It's almost a ritual with them. They enjoy bargaining. Now I'll start in earnest."

The man gave a price, and Vic raised his eyes to heaven in shocked surprise, half turning away. The seller then reduced his figure as Vic asked Alex which two she really wanted. Alex considered a moment and rather slowly said, in Spanish, "Maybe these two," indicating her choice.

Vic leaned against the post of the makeshift stand and asked if there would be a reduction if they bought two of them. The man gave another price, and so began another bargaining session. At last, they hit on a figure that was about half the original price. As the seller carefully wrapped the pots in newspaper, he assured them that at this rate he would soon go out of business.

"Things have gone up, you know," he reminded them with a brilliant smile. "I'm having a hard time!"

"I know—things are bad all over," Vic replied, burdening himself with the two enormous beaten-brass containers.

They moved slowly through the crowd, Alex keeping close behind Vic, until they emerged at the end of the double lane of stands. She watched his broad shoulders as they passed housewives and running children. How easily he walked along, the tallest figure in the area, fitting in so well, with his sunburned face and arms, his blue shirt and jeans modest but fitting perfectly. And now that he and Marga had an understanding, she would never tell him that it was all over between Con and herself, truce or no truce.

"We may just as well eat lunch here," he said, turning to her. "Pepe's busy with the engine, and I told him not to bother with anything else. What would you like to eat?"

"Anything at all," she said, so relaxed in his company that it really didn't matter.

"There's a great taco place on the other side of town," he suggested. "And the *caldo de pollo*'s rich. Chicken soup, to you.. Want to try it?"

He had known instinctively that it was what she most wanted at the moment. Few places made really good tacos, where one could see the meat rolling around on a spit, dripping its juices, which often went into the consommé.

An hour later, after a brief session with Vic's barber, during which Alex waited on a bench outside, reading an old magazine, they ate at the taco place, sitting again at a table outside on the tree-lined street. As she dug into the warm tortillas rolled around crisp chunks of delicious pork, she reveled in a cool sea breeze that tempered the tropical sun, glinting down through the trees. Around them humble workers stopping for their midday meal ate, chatting, laughing and occasionally toasting one another with glasses of beer, all of which created an almost festive atmosphere. Alex's knee accidentally brushed against Vic's under the table, and she decided to let it rest there. She dreaded the passing of the sun in the sky, the shifting shadows, for they all taunted her with the fact that this magic day was drawing to a close.

When they returned to the square, they found a small carnival—set up, it seemed, at a moment's notice. The performers advertising it were giving short exhibitions on the street, surrounded by admiring children and passers-by. Alex and Vic stopped to watch, and Vic bought ices for them from a roving vendor.

It was late when they climbed into the jeep and headed back to San Pablo. The day had gone like a dream—Alex felt happy, yet incomplete at the same time. How easy it would be to love Vic forever, she thought as they careened around the mountainside. As they drove, the sun slowly sank into the sea, burnishing the moving waves a deep orange that melted into red.

"It's fantastic," Vic commented, glancing at the ocean. "Is there anything like this in California?" He looked at her directly and she shivered, having forgotten the way his searching gaze could affect her... almost burn into her.

"Oh, we have beautiful scenery too," she assured him dryly. As his dark eyes continued to flick back to her from the road, Alex felt herself glow golden inside, molten like the rays of the sinking sun.

All of a sudden he turned off the main road, directing the jeep down a rough trail. She did not have to ask him where they were going.

When the orange-red horizon, brighter than the Mayan gods whose images had ruled this land so many centuries ago, was in front of them, he stopped the jeep. Still not speaking, they got out and walked toward the sea, but unlike their easy camaraderie in town, there was now a different, deeper feeling between them, an elemental bond that was somehow part of the deserted ancient beach receiving the sun's last gifts of the day, and the rhythm of the pounding surf.

They settled beside each other on the sand, still not touching.

"I must admit"—she finally broke the silence—"that perhaps California isn't quite the same as this."

"The same or not," he replied, "I suppose you'll be going out there again?"

She was sensitive to the intended implication. He wanted to know if she and Conrad would be reestablishing their home there when they remarried. She found herself not wanting him to know whether or not she would remarry Con.

"Nothing is decided yet," she said, hedging. "And your own plans? After you announce your find?"

"Well, I'll be pretty busy with the two governments," he said. "On such a project there's lots of red tape to go through. First it'll be roped off—declared a national treasure. Then my learned society in New York will arrange an expedition. We'll get permission from the *Instituto Nacional de Antropología y Historia*, and maybe a joint expedition with all the necessary equipment will be organized by both nations. And all the while I'll be fending off reporters from a million newspapers."

"Yes, of course all that," she said, noting how he had avoided mentioning his personal plans. It was typical, his probing into her life, with the veil of privacy drawn over his relationship with Marga.

"You will have contributed an important discovery to your profession, then," she said, remembering Ed's telling her that Vic wouldn't marry until he had done this.

"Right you are," he said. "And that means everything to me. I'll finally feel free—free to pay more attention to my personal life."

Her heart sank. Of course this meant that he would marry—and marry Marga.

Again they sat in silence, but the feeling between them spoke without words, spoke louder than the sound of the waves breaking against the shore. Then he turned to her, his warm eyes probing hers, searing into her very soul. She felt his hand on the back of her neck and reveled in the way he gently massaged her, then moved his fingers sensuously down her spine. Her love for him was right, she knew, more right than anything.

She turned to his lips and lost herself. Suddenly he was embracing her, and she slid her arms around him, drawing him closer with a joyous freedom made sweeter by long restraint. Gently she moved her hands up and down the length of his strong back, caressing him the way she'd always longed to caress him.

The world disappeared, the world and all her cares,

as he gently lowered her onto the sand and they began to move together. All the love she felt for him now flowed out of her, through the fingers that shyly, tentatively touched him, through the lips that tenderly opened to him, through the breasts that strained to be free for him. She loved him with a passion that overwhelmed her. And as he returned her passion, kiss for kiss, caress for caress, she gave herself up to a spell woven by the surging waves, the melting sun and the mysterious Mayan ruins.

CHAPTER TWELVE

SHE WAS ALONE.

The two blouses hanging on the outside of her closet door along with the two hand-embroidered dresses only depressed her as she remembered under what joyful circumstances she had bought them. She placed them out of sight, in the closet. The clear, sharp underwater photographs drying on the improvised clothesline in the bathroom did nothing to alleviate her mood. Just when she should have felt happier than she ever had, it was as though the bottom had fallen out of the supports of her life. A little more diving time, and it would soon be over. She would be reading about it in various periodicals, looking at pictures the new photographers on the expedition would take, seeing Vic's picture here and there; then, maybe on the social pages, reading of his marriage.

Her eyes fell on her emergency bottle of brandy on the bottom shelf of her night table. On impulse she snatched it up and splashed a double shot into a glass. She thought she couldn't feel any worse. What if she did have a hangover in the morning? What difference did anything make, after all? Vic and Marga were probably at dinner, laughing, talking and clinking glasses with Ed, Don and Jill.

Who was thinking about her, alone, with no dinner,

and practically ignored by the only man in the world who meant anything at all to her? The thought that she herself had decided not to join them did not help the matter at all. Vic or Ed or somebody should have insisted or come to get her.

In this self-indulgent mood she finished developing her pictures, barely glancing at the attractive results. Then she prepared for bed, searched for the new novel she had remembered to buy in Tierra Quemada and arranged her pillows comfortably for reading. Thank goodness she had bought a mystery, and a scary one. She was drawn into the story more and more, until a knock on the door startled her, and she realized that she had subconsciously heard an approaching motor.

Throwing on a robe, she looked out the curtains, to see the jeep in front. She opened the door, to find Vic standing there with a large thin pizza box held carefully in both hands.

"I thought you might need a little nourishment," he said, his smile devastating. Of course he wouldn't just leave you, you fool, she reprimanded herself. "Ed and the gang started to come to drag you out to eat, but I explained you had some developing to do. They are worried that you don't want to eat with them anymore."

All the earlier unkind thoughts about her friends melted, and she felt better about things in general. And strangely enough, as Vic opened the steaming pizza, she became ravenously hungry.

"Thanks," she murmured. "I'd love a piece."

"I had to beg the pizza-maker in town to reheat his

oven," he continued. "Naturally, he had closed up around seven."

She sat down and began to eat. "I've got some pretty good shots drying," she said. "You can look at them, but don't smear them."

He did not move. "Alex," he said, and she trembled to hear the tenderness in his voice. "Alex, we can't act as if nothing has happened. We have to talk."

She turned around in her chair and looked up at him, her eyes filling with tears. "I know," she replied.

"Look, Alex, I know I've been a drudge for a long time. I'm aware that I've allowed very little time for play in my life, that for a lot of reasons it's been work, work, work."

She found she could not speak. All she could do was nod, feeling nervous inside. What was he trying to tell her?

"You know that I'm a sort of black sheep in my family, and I've come to realize that that's partly why this find means so much to me. One mention of this in the Boston *Globe* or the *New York Times*, and my family will respect my work the way I do."

She continued to look at him, almost frozen by the turmoil within her. Would he finally admit that he loved her?

But his next words disappointed her. "You're a talented woman," he said. "I really don't know how the work would have gone without you."

It seemed as if he wanted to say more, but he suddenly turned and walked over to look at the pictures. "I don't blame you for getting your special film from

California," he said as he replaced the prints carefully on the line. "As I've told you about your other pictures, these are some of the best shots I've seen."

"I know," she agreed, forcing her voice to be calm. "I just hope the other photographers you have on the expedition will use the same slow film. It's finer-grained, to give that extra detail."

"Too bad you won't be in on the expedition," he said, sitting down, and her heart sank. So he was just trying to tell her goodbye, to let her down easy. "Guess you'll be in that California hacienda," he continued.

"What California hacienda?" she asked, surprised.

"The one you'll share with your husband—I mean your ex-husband—when you remarry," he answered, watching her closely.

Caught in a dilemma, she answered with a faint, "I told you nothing's been decided yet."

"It shouldn't take too much thinking out," he went on, "from what I could see. Ex-husband sees his mistake, follows ex-wife to the ends of the earth—in this case, San Pablo—rides in on his prancing charger—in this case a snappy Masarati—gets ex-wife's promise to remarry as soon as her diving stint's over with old, fuddy-duddy archeologist. Spends the night just like old times, and roars off in the morning with everything settled."

"It wasn't like that at all!" she cried out, vexed at the picture he described.

He rose as if to leave. "Then I suppose I saw two ghosts at the window. And I didn't see his car at all the next morning. It was a mirage, right?"

"What right do you have to criticize me in the first

place?" she demanded, facing him across the table. "Even if that's true, what do you have to do with it?" She felt a rising anger. "And if you think you can criticize me—well, I'm *me* and you're *you* off the boat, remember? I would have thought that that meant on the beach, too!"

To her surprise, he flushed beneath his deep tan and came around the table to catch her arm. Before she realized it, she was in his arms, being kissed slowly, deliberately, held in a grip from which there was no escape. Through her thin summer robe she felt his hard body against hers and knew the same surging flame it always gave her. There was no time to think as his demanding kisses increased. In the surging emotions now overwhelming her she lost all sense of proportion as time stood still. As before, she was lost in his caresses, and after the first shock and surprise, barely realized she was acceding, then forced by him and her own body to acquiesce. In a fever of pent-up passion and frustration she clung to him as his hands, more gentle now, traveled the length of her body, searching, caressing, possessing. There were no barriers between them as she yielded to his love-making, responding with a passion as primitive as that of the flamenco dancer, and as unfettered. There was nothing between them but the raw need for each other, a need she wanted more than ever to be realized . . . assuaged.

Had yesterday really happened, she asked herself, or had it just been one of her dreams come to life? Sitting up in bed, she looked around the room. The clock showed six, and she was alone. Suddenly the entire scene of the night before swept over her, and she buried her head in the pillow, angry and dismayed. Twice they had made love, and each time it had been wonderful for both of them. Each time, caught up in passion, she had been sure that Vic loved her as she loved him. But once again she was alone. And once again, she realized, they had failed to come to an understanding, failed to express in words what they really felt for each other. They had argued, and their anger had turned to something else, and despite the momentous step they had taken, they were no closer to a true commitment. Was he only using her after all? Would he go back to Marga?

Then she remembered his insistent references to Conrad. Could he possibly be jealous? Yet there were some men who, when dealing with two women in different contexts, were jealous of both of them. Was it that? Or was he indeed sincere?

Sheer habit made her rise to prepare for the dive, though she went through her usual routine dazed and wondering, swinging from one conclusion to its opposite. As she got in her car and headed for the pier, noting the jeep had already gone, she was determined to take a stand, without knowing exactly how she would begin.

Pepe was on deck as she approached, looking at the sky and then out to sea. Vic was nowhere in sight.

"I'm not too sure about the weather," he greeted her. "It doesn't look like a storm, but just the same it's not quite normal."

For once, she had forgotten to check the weather

when she arose. That, she knew, was the measure of her confusion.

"But there's no dark water," she replied, looking into the ocean as she boarded.

"No, but there's something a little different," he insisted. "And when I passed my neighbors' house on the way—the Barreras—I noticed their chickens were nowhere in sight. They were still roosting."

"What's that got to do with anything, Pepe?" she asked, amused.

"Surely you know the reaction of animals has a lot to do with everything," he said seriously. "For instance, when you're diving and the big groupers suddenly disappear, you know there's a shark about, or something big and just as dangerous."

"Yes, but the chickens?" she insisted.

"Same thing," he replied. "And my dog didn't follow me out to the gate this morning, either, now that I think of it. He stayed under the table."

Still unimpressed, Alex went around the deck to recheck her wet suit, wondering when she could have a talk with Vic without Pepe's presence. There can't be any more of this, she reasoned. She didn't understand him, and would refuse to be hurt again—by anyone. At the breakfast call, she went into the salon, to find Vic sitting at the table, staring into space. Pepe was still in the galley.

"Alex, I'm sorry," he began in a low voice, in English. "I never meant to act the way I did. Your ex-husband's coming back for you, and I had no right to make love to you like that."

"What in the world are you talking about, Vic?" she interrupted, quite unaware that Pepe was now setting the table. "I don't understand you at all!"

"And I don't understand you, Alex," he replied quickly. "I thought we'd eventually wind up together in spite of everything. I know—I know—" he waved down her incipient protest, "I was antagonistic at the beginning—rude, almost. That's because I knew from the very beginning—when you got off that plane—that I wanted you. And I didn't want anything to interfere with my dive! I tried to push you out of my mind—even got closer to Marga to try—but it was useless. I can't seem to stay away from you."

A surging tide of happiness rose in her. Could it be possible? His words came out of her fondest dreams.

"And when I saw you through that window, kissing Conrad—"

"He was kissing me—I never responded," she murmured.

"I was furious! Then I knew I had no right to be angry—after all, I was the one who'd insisted that we lead separate lives off the *Vera*. And I figured that Conrad came here to get you back."

"But he didn't succeed," she said, now floating on her full tide of joy. She wanted to reach across the table and lay her head against his chest, stripped to the waist as he was in swim shorts.

"But his car stayed there all night," he said accusingly to her. The full impact of his jealousy at last came to her, and suddenly she felt free to tell him everything.

"But he stayed on the floor—in his sleeping bag," she clarified.

"His sleeping bag? On the floor?" He looked dazedly at her.

"Con's still a playboy. I don't know why I married him in the first place. Yes, since there aren't any hotels or motels nearby, he asked permission to sleep in the house. After all, it was late. I didn't tell you earlier—I guess I was just using Con's presence to try to get back at you."

"And if I used anybody, it was Marga," he reflected. "I never promised her anything at all. But when I felt attracted to you or was jealous of you, I tried to get closer to her to balance it—to wipe you from my mind."

"And did you succeed?" she asked, trying to remain calm, with the singing in her ears.

"Hell, no!" he exploded, rising, and sitting down beside her.

Neither had noticed Pepe's discreet withdrawal, nor the fragrant smell of fresh coffee brewing.

"Alex," he said huskily, "if you're not going back to your ex-husband, could you—would you—" He paused, taking her face in his hands and kissing her.

"Could I, would I?" she questioned later, drawing away.

"Marry me, of course!" he almost shouted, now seeming sure of the answer.

"Yes, yes!" she cried, filled with happiness as he drew her toward him again to kiss her tenderly. It was then that she knew how long she had loved him, much longer than she had thought. Beyond that physical magnetism he projected, she was drawn to his sense of purpose and dedication, and to his quiet strength.

"Of course, I can't give you Masaratis." He smiled.

"It doesn't make any difference," she replied. "As a matter of fact, I think a jeep is much more my speed."

He laughed. "And nothing makes any difference to me as long as you say we'll be together the rest of our lives." He rose, pulled her up and kissed her again, then pulled her toward the galley.

"Pepe," he said with an arm around her, "congratulate us; we're going to get married!"

"Of course. I knew that long ago," Pepe replied, pouring coffee. "But now *you* know it, correct?"

They laughed together, remembering Pepe's cryptic proverbs.

"I hope this pot of coffee didn't get spoiled from sitting too long." He smiled at them, placing two cups on the table, then turned and gave each of them the abrazo of congratulation.

Alex ate, not tasting anything in her complete joy, which was with Vic. One of his strong hands kept one of hers engaged across the table, his glance seeking hers repeatedly as his hand tightened. Pepe diplomatically found work to do in the galley.

"We have plans to make—lots of them," Vic said as they finally rose to go on deck. "We'll be a team on the expedition. You'll share everything with me, since you were in almost from the beginning. And you'll be in charge of all the photography. . . ."

Alex felt so happy that she couldn't even think about the future—all that mattered was now. Yet what was most precious to him, he was willing to share with her . . . the ultimate gift—the ultimate gift of love. She could barely answer as she left him to change.

"Don't stay down too long," Pepe said as they later waited to flip over. "I don't like the looks of the weather."

"But the sun is out," Vic said, peering at the sky. "There's no sign of a storm."

Pepe shook his head doubtfully, and Alex surmised that he was still thinking of the chickens unaccountably roosting.

Shortly after, she and Vic were walking on the ocean floor, with the dive promising to be productive. Fragmented remains of old water- and sand-polished stones still clinging to what had once been buildings and were now almost rubble had to be photographed from all sides. They floated into the maze of the crooked streets, trying to get enough information to make a crude map of the city.

Never had she been so happy on a dive, or anywhere else. The murky depths assumed an endearing aspect for her, especially when they came to life in subdued colors under her lights. And when she would come back on the expedition with Vic to direct the photography, she would know her way. They'd be a true team!

Besides keeping a eye out for danger, which might be buried in any part of the sandy bottom uncovered by the crude paving stones, she scanned the area for pieces of encrusted mud that might turn out to be valuable artifacts giving clues . . . now that she had learned to identify them. She even gave thought to going back to the university to learn more about land archeology, if time permitted. And what might they not accomplish when the expedition got underway with the right equipment, the expensive vacuum hoses, and air lifts?

A barracuda passed by, and seemed to be moving hastily, and Alex suddenly realized that it was the first fish she had seen on the dive, when there were usually so many—some inquisitive, others threatening but usually retreating when convinced they were meant no harm.

Suddenly Alex felt the water around her begin to vibrate, feeling first her eardrums buzzing and then her whole body shaking. Vic had been leading the way, in front of her, and she saw him turn toward her and give the danger signal. He approached her as fast as the water and now-shifting sand would allow and unfastened her weight belt, then moved to unfasten his own. She glanced at her air-pressure gauge, thinking for a moment that her air tank had ruptured, but a quick inspection assured her that this was not the case.

More and more she seemed to be swimming in sand, and barely missed the cave-in of one of the remnants of the wall she had just finished photographing. Vic was now reaching for her, but she could hardly see him, with the sand avalanche between them. She reached out for his extended arms and was anguished to be drawn back from him with a pulling force not to be resisted. She had no time to wonder what had happened. The undersea world seemed to be coming to an end, as she was caught in a small whirlpool and tossed in and out of its suction.

She pushed back panic as the nightmare continued. Her world had gone crazy; she could not see anything of Vic. She drew back in horror as an octopus was spewed out of its lair in front of her, writhing and protesting, trailing its ink. She felt herself rising, then sinking, and the ocean bottom seemed to rise and sink with her during the brief flashes when she could identify it. Then began an eerie sound, pulsing through the water at irregular intervals—a sound more frightening than the turmoil she was caught up in. Once she thought she saw Vic through the opaque murk, but his form soon disappeared. To have found him and lost him so soon, she thought. It was clear that the kind of happiness she had so briefly known was too intense to last.

Myriad forms of tossed-about sea life passed, sometimes bumping into her on all sides. Then the ocean seemed to be caught up in another convulsion as one enormous body of water appeared to crash against an opposing body, whirling her upward. She now knew she was enduring an underwater earthquake, being shunted up or down at nature's whim. There came a momentary lull in the violent motion, and she caught the signal from her J valve that her air pressure had dropped to three hundred pounds. Immediately she pulled the lever to release the remaining three hundred pounds, but knew that she had only from five to fifteen more minutes' remaining air before she must reach the surface—wherever that was. She thought of the walls of limestone and coral, hardened by centuries, and knew that even if she could see them, it would be impossible to avoid them in the thrashing, angry sea now blackening rapidly with shifting sand.

She thought of Vic, hoping he too had pulled the lever of his valve, knowing the time left on their air supply would coincide. Then she began to pray that he was still alive and that they both would survive this onslaught. What had happened to the secret city, she dared not imagine.

The sea still boiled, and rendered all within it helpless. Alex, now giving herself over to it, ceasing to struggle, thought it must be a dream—a nightmare. She would wake up in her little casita, and it would all be gone. Yet a small core of consciousness told her of her danger, her small chance of surviving unless she surfaced.

She vaguely knew that she was pulled into another sucking whirlpool, down into the center, or was it up into the center—how could she tell? She collided at one point with something solid—soft, thank God, but solid, perhaps a live thing.

Was she getting drowsy now, or was she losing consciousness? She tried to rally her forces but was finally made to surrender after gradually losing the fight. She knew she was still getting air, but had no idea of time or space. She felt that an eternity had passed since the beginning of the earthquake. She was so tired . . . she would just close her eyes and sleep for a few minutes. . . .

CHAPTER THIRTEEN

HER EYES OPENED to gray skies, and she tried to remember where she was. It was difficult, as the sea was frothing. If the waves would only calm, she knew she would remember her name and what she was doing so alone, floating on her back. Her air supply suddenly stopped, and she automatically tore off her face plate and harness, breathing in fresh, pure air. But what in the world was she doing there, and where were her cameras?

A streak of lightning zigzagged across the sky, and a distant growl of thunder came at her. But she didn't care much. It was so pleasant floating, going along at random with the surging waves, most of which washed over her with a muted roar. She would just rest awhile and wait until later to decide what it was all about. She was a little tired. She shut her eyes.

Somebody was disturbing her rest, roughly clasping her under her chin and pulling her along backward. She was being towed and was unable to turn around to catch sight of the person who would not release her. Tall whitecaps rimming the choppy waves broke in her face as she and her unseen captor made what seemed to be very slow progress. The sea looked lopsided. As she tried to turn her head again she was firmly repulsed, the hand under her chin demanding absolute obedience. Oh, well, she'd just as soon allow herself to rest a little more. . . .

As she climbed the ladder of the boat, her memory returned full force. My God! she thought. She had managed to survive! That hard hand under her chin was Vic's hand, and he was right behind her, helping her to mount. Dripping and coming out of her daze, now mercifully conscious of all that had happened, she was taken aboard by a waiting Pepe. Joy and relief flooded back as she turned to reach out for Vic—a miraculously whole Vic, now stepping on board. Silently he enfolded her in his arms for a moment before releasing her to begin briskly tapping her cheeks.

"Are you all right? How do you feel?" he kept asking.

She felt her circulation returning, and he began to work on her hands, chafing and massaging them.

"I'm fine," she replied, then collapsed again onto his chest.

"Then let's get that wet suit off right away and give you a good, rough toweling. Thank God you're safe!" He headed her toward the cabin.

"But what—was it a quake?" she asked, reluctant to leave the deck.

"The radio says it was a small underwater quake and sand shift," Pepe replied.

"A *small* quake!" Alex exclaimed.

"No quake's small when you're in the middle of it!" Vic said, leading her off. "God! I might have lost you!" He said, embracing her as they entered the cabin. "And just when I had found you!"

"I—I thought the same thing down under there,"

she stammered, holding him tight. "But I'm getting you all wet!" She drew away, and he quickly helped her off with her suit as he talked.

"Pepe saw me floating face down, after running the boat around in circles to keep it from capsizing, and he anchored and free-dived to pull me out. When I came to I thought for sure I'd lost you. It was ages before you surfaced."

"But Vic—what about the secret city?"

"I never thought of it till now! Just you! I guess it's gone under. It was an avalanche of a sand shift."

"But Vic—all your work—what about your announcement?"

"Alex—it simply doesn't matter. You're safe—and I'm safe! All your photos and the artifacts will support the find, and at least I know it's down there. Pepe and I still have a fix on it."

Alex toweled herself dry, happy for both of them. Yet thoughts of the now doubly lost city shadowed that happiness. Back up on deck, they found Pepe preparing to take off in the rough sea, presumably for their pier in San Pablo.

"I hate to see the site covered up like that," he said to Vic, "but down this way, that's what happens sometimes."

"I know—I know. I guess it's the same thing that came about when the city first got inundated, centuries ago." Vic sighed, resigned. "An earthquake or seaquake, it probably triggered a gigantic tidal wave plus the sand shift. That's what my expedition would have found out."

Pepe, looking depressed, left to start up the motor,

leaving them with his battery-powered radio tuned to the Tierra Quemada station.

They were leaning over the rail, examining the sky, which was now miraculously turning from gray to blue—a rain-washed blue with the promise of bright sunshine. Vic's arm was around Alex, so that she felt completely protected, almost making her forget the recent nightmare they had undergone.

"Pepe's taking the other route," Vic commented. "I wonder if he thinks we need a sight-seeing tour."

"I'd just as soon," Alex replied. "We can see the effect of the quake all along the coast. And I hope it didn't destroy the coral reef you showed me, where I got those wonderful shots. But Vic, isn't there any chance of salvaging anything of our city back there?"

"It'll take another dive to tell, but I doubt it," he replied.

"I'll go with you. I lost one of my cameras, but I have my other one back at the casita. And another set of lights."

"After a quake like this, there might be a resettlement of the sand," he pointed out. "We'd have to wait a while. But Alex—forget the city!" He held her away from him, only to pull her back again. "I've got you! I almost lost you, but I have you back again!"

"I forgot to thank you for saving my life," she said when he finally released her.

"Any time at all." He grinned, pulled her to a deck chair and sat down beside her.

"I'm surprised we didn't lose these in the holocaust," he said, indicating the chairs. "And I never asked you if you got hurt anywhere—if anything hit you in the water."

"I don't think so. I'm fine—just tired. I tried to surface but never knew which way was up."

"I should have taken off your weight belt with one hand and held onto you with the other," he lamented. "We got separated right away. But never again! We never will be separated!"

She looked at him and smiled. Even after what she had gone through, she began to feel the attraction of his body, now stretched out so close to hers. He could have been a bronze god from some earlier era—Mercury, or Apollo. The firm, hard muscles rippled beneath the tanned skin. Was she under the spell of some Mayan god—Chacmul, perhaps? Whoever cast the spell, she was captured in it, and she knew that she was captured forever. There could be nobody else for her.

"Alex," he said, catching her hand in his, "when I was down there swirling around, the only thing I kept repeating to myself was that I had never told you I love you. But I do—you know that, don't you?"

She looked at him and as usual felt his gaze bore into her with its devastating effect. But now she had no need to fight it. They belonged to each other.

"Yes, and I love you too, Vic," she answered as he bent over to kiss her again.

Pepe had set a slow pace with the *Vera*, giving them a chance to examine the coastline and the ocean for the effects of the recent upheaval. Alex could detect nothing unusual on either sea or land, and Vic told her that in Greece he had often been told of isolated upheavals which did little, if any, damage. It was just that being caught up in the center of one made it seem as though the end of the world had come.

"It's possible that the gang on shore hasn't even heard about it on the radio—they're so busy at the plant."

"I guess unless there are casualties, it seems minor," Alex agreed.

The boat slowed to a gentle stop. The seas had calmed as the sky cleared and a brilliant sun came out. It was as though nothing had happened.

Pepe dropped anchor, and they realized that they were at the site of the sunken city.

"Wonder what's up," Vic said as they watched Pepe strip to his swim shorts and free-dive. He reminded her of the younger Pepe she had seen in the home movies, so gracefully did he dive from the rail.

"I can't imagine his wanting to swim today," Vic commented.

"He might want to let off steam," Alex replied. "He's been under a lot of pressure—keeping the boat afloat and diving for you..."

As they waited, they watched gulls drifting over the waves, and small boats in the distance draw nearer the shoreline.

Finally they heard Pepe emerging from the water and climbing the ladder to the deck. Alex marveled at his transformation. His face was glowing almost angelically, as though he had witnessed a holy miracle at some shrine. He seemed wreathed in crystal droplets of water, which shone in the sun as they fell on deck. He said nothing but beckoned them to the rail.

Wonderingly they obeyed him as he pointed downward. They bent over to focus on the rippling surface, strangely clear, in view of the recent cataclysm. It took awhile to accustom their eyes to the sun's reflection, but gradually Pepe's discovery was revealed to them. The outlines of the city rose almost whole, unencumbered by the sand which had preserved it for centuries. Even from that distance, they could recognize the symmetry of the remembered coral-tipped outlines, now more visible as walls. Had it risen with the upheaval of the sea bed? Or had the protecting sand simply revealed it while at the same time covering the other part of the city with its slanting avalanche?

At first Alex felt she had retreated into her dreamlike state—how could this be possible? Was it a mirage? But no, Pepe had free-dived down into it. Vic was now holding her—apparently too moved to speak. She turned at the same time he did and looked at him, not trusting herself to comment. Was the clear water—after the turbulent quake—a symbol for them? They were to have both the city and each other. Their good fortune was not to be believed.

Overwhelmed, they remained silent, clinging to each other.

Pepe went to lift anchor, softly humming. Later Alex heard him improvising in song what she recognized as his favorite message to them. "Man proposes and God disposes." But the only thing she could think of was the clear water—and the Mayan gods, who indeed had been watching out for them.

Don't miss any of these breathless tales of lovers lost and found! Order today!

FLAMENCO NIGHTS #1
by Susanna Collins
In the Cordoba of gold-hued days and soft, jasmine-scented nights artist Rosie Powell risks heartbreak again when she falls in love with world-famous flamenco guitarist—and notorious womanizer—Juan de Arévalo.

WINTER LOVE SONG #2
by Meredith Kingston
Ski Champion Felicia Hollingsworth, still desperately in love with her former coach and husband, Grant Mitchell, meets him again on Sun Valley's seductive slopes. Can she return to his life and not his arms—the place claimed by another woman?

THE CHADBOURNE LUCK #3
by Lucia Curzon
The dazzling Lady Celia Chadbourne has a score to settle with the darkly handsome Lord Armin Sherlay. But in a risky play of hearts, passion becomes sweeter than revenge...

OUT OF A DREAM #4
by Jennifer Rose
A dashing ad agency executive and a devastatingly handsome architect vie for Eileen Connor on a glamour assignment in Switzerland.

GLITTER GIRL #5
by Jocelyn Day
Divorced, beautiful, Tiffany Harte returns to Cougar Beach on the rugged Oregon coast and faces the scornful contempt of her first real love, Clay.